Revolt
The King's Knight
Book 1

J.A. IRONSIDE

Published in 2019 by Sharpe Books.

CONTENTS

A knyght ther was, and that a worthy man,
That fro the tyme that he first bigan
To riden out, he loved chivalrie
Trouthe and honour, fredom and curteisie
Ful worthy was he in his lordes werre,
And thereto hadde he riden, no man ferre,
As wel in Cristendom as in Hethenesse,
And evere honoured for his worthynesse.
—Geoffrey Chaucer, The Canterbury Tales:
The General Prologue

1.

The persistent, metallic ringing echoed inside Gregory Maudesley's skull, fracturing his thoughts into sharp, nonsensical shards. He supposed he must be near a smithy, although he couldn't remember why. Had he been unhorsed at a joust? He hadn't the faintest recollection of falling, nor indeed, of the last time he'd entered a tourney. God's Blood, his head ached.

"...He never yet no villainy said, in all his life unto no manner wight..."

The words were spoken with wry pleasure, forming a soft counterpoint to the harsh thumping in his skull. Gregory blinked and groaned, screwing his eyes shut against the blades of sunlight that sliced into his head. The inside of his mouth tasted like he'd spent a night licking the cellar floor in a tavern of low repute. Sundry other aches and pains added themselves to the list clamouring for his attention. He scrubbed a hand over his face and realised his hand was wet. That he was, in fact, soaked to the skin and cold from the breast bone down.

"...He was a verray parfit gentil knight..."

He ignored the voice in favour of beating his brain into action. Had he suffered a mortal wound? He forced his eyes open just as a long, brown, indignant muzzle thrust itself at him, blowing grass scented breath into his face.

"Get away," Gregory croaked, shoving ineffectually at the horse. The horse snorted, showing yellowed teeth before nudging at him again. He assumed it wanted a drink and objected to him being sprawled in its trough. How in God's name had he got here?

Gregory turned his head to gaze with bleary-eyed annoyance at whichever ponce thought now was a good time for declaiming in verse. "Will you just shut up. I bloody hate poetry."

1

The 'poet' was middling man – middling height, middling build, middling brown hair and beard. An ordinary fellow of around forty or so. He smiled slyly at Gregory, as if they shared a secret, transforming his pale, ascetic face with an expression of uncanny glee. Gregory found himself perturbed by that shrewd, dark gaze.

"You can stop smiling like that while you're at it."

"My apologies, sir knight. The circumstances were such that my muse made an unexpected appearance. I was quite unable to resist." The poet's mouth was tucked up at the corners behind his beard.

Gregory was certain he was being mocked. Gritting his teeth against the sick headache, he gripped the sides of the trough and heaved himself out to stand dripping and none too sweet smelling in the mud. The brown horse barged Gregory aside to get to the trough and he almost slipped. He recognised the yard outside *The Crossed Keys* now. It had been a favourite haunt of his brother's, back in the days when William was young and roistering, not to mention alive. Gregory had never been part of the clientele though. Not until last night. His head chose that moment to throb hard enough to make him retch. Saint Vincent's sacred ball sac, how much ale had he drunk?

"You have all your limbs, at least," the poet offered.

"Any reason I shouldn't?" Gregory stamped life back into his feet. His clothes were ruined, not that they had been particularly fine before. More concerning was the thundering, sick pain and the way his vision kept doubling. He didn't believe it was entirely down to ale. One of his molars felt loose when he ran an exploratory tongue against the inside of his tender jaw. A stab in his side suggested cracked ribs. And hadn't he been carrying something important?

"A better question might be how you came to bed down in a horse trough," the poet observed. He seemed determined to be as unhelpful as possible.

"I was drunk, not that it's any business of yours. Have you nothing better to do, you old sod?"

It was a rhetorical question, but the poet answered anyway. "It seemed to me, that there might well be nothing better to do,

2

than to see whether a man who was in his cups enough to barely feel a serious beating, would ever wake. I have enjoyed good service at this tavern on many occasions. It would have been a sore pity to pollute the yard with such a large, ungainly corpse as you would have made."

"Beaten?" Gregory picked out the one word of importance.

"Robbed too, by all accounts."

Memories of the previous night crashed through his pounding head. Gregory swore with a fluency that made the poet's eyebrows climb towards his cap.

"I stand before a master of the craft, and I a mere novice," the poet said in reply.

Gregory held on to his temper with effort. He didn't usually strike men who could not fight back. Not without reason, anyway, but the poet was trying his limited supply of patience. And the money... He cast around vainly for the saddlebacks containing his hard won coin, but they were gone. His horse? Gregory lifted his head sharply and the world swayed in a nauseating ripple. Drum was standing across the yard, under a row of hawthorns.

"Your horse declined to accompany them," the poet said drily. "They must have been desperate or foolish to attempt to steal such a beast."

True enough. Gregory had never been able to afford a destrier but then few knights could. Drum was unusually fine even for a courser, and a big, black horse drew attention. The thieves must be beyond foolish. Stupid enough to follow a knight and set upon him, when he went outside to take a piss.

"What happened to my groom?" Gregory thought aloud.

"Was that the fellow with the two amblers? According to the stable lad, he went with the thieves. As did your packhorses."

So his groom had either thrown his lot in with the thieves, or had been working with them all along. Most likely the latter. What were the chances that a gang of robbers just happened upon Gregory when he'd had a skinful and his braies were down?

"Which way did they go?" Gregory said.

"I'm only lately arrived. I saw nothing." The poet pursed his

3

mouth as if tasting his words before he uttered them. "The proprietor of this fine establishment might know more, if you can circumvent his impenetrable stupidity enough to acquire answers. T'was he who reported that a man had died in the horse trough after taking a club to the head." Correctly reading Gregory's expression, the poet went on. "The word is that a party of men headed north, into the forest–"

Gregory cursed and kicked the side of the horse trough. The brown horse startled sideways, casting a reproachful look at him.

"Hold, friend," the poet said. "If they have not holed up somewhere, they will have to pass the town of Littlefolds. And one of the thieves had a very recognisable scarred face. Or so the innkeeper said."

Gregory considered hauling the innkeeper out here and dunking him in the trough until he explained how he'd allowed a noble to be robbed in his inn yard. "Littlefolds is not in Wynnstree?"

"On the border between Hinckford and Suffolk. After robbing a knight, I imagine they were keen to leave one demesne and hide in another. Though it says something about the current state of lawlessness in Wynnstee that they felt bold enough to do it," the poet said.

Gregory couldn't argue with that. The Maudesley lands had been without a lord for too long and these were troubled times.

"I see you do not intend to engage a local constable," the poet observed. "If you find your thieves, what do you intend to do with them?"

Gregory smiled without mirth, the expression ferocious enough that the poet took a step back. "I'll request the return of my property. The rest is in God's hands."

"I see." The poet seemed to resolve some internal conflict. "The best of luck to you, then."

Gregory's mind was already on retrieving his blades from the tavern strong room.

The poet smiled faintly. "A question, before you go?"

"Ask," Gregory snapped.

"What put you so far in your cups as to come to such

4

misadventure?"

"What possible interest can that be to you?"

"I write from life. A death, perhaps?"

"A wedding," Gregory growled. "I got married recently."

"Ah," the poet said. "That explains everything."

2.

18th March, 1381
Twelve Weeks Earlier

By the time Gregory discovered he was the sole surviving heir to the Maudesley estate, his father and William had been dead for over a year. He'd left Italy immediately, having put down as few roots in Florence as he had in Spain or France or any of the dozen other places he'd lived in the last eight years. Gregory's means, on returning to England, were slender. His courser was good, but no longer in the first flush of his youth. He'd had a palfrey too but the wretched thing had gone lame on the road. His armour was simple and had seen better days, despite his meticulous care of it. On more than one occasion, Gregory had concluded that he'd have had more success as a mercenary if he were more flexible in his attitude to authority. But few men were worth following – none at all unless you were well compensated.

Gregory lacked William's ability to appear to yield with grace, without ever leaving the issuer of a command in any doubt of his natural superiority. William, the golden, older brother, the heir, favourite of their father and flower of knightly virtue. At least if you didn't fall foul of any of his darker pursuits. As long as you weren't competition. Well-favoured, athletic, naturally charismatic William. Gregory had been loyal to his brother. Had admired him and looked up to him.

But no one is truly golden. If Gregory had learned anything as a mercenary, it was that there were no depths to which men would not sink in their own interests. His brother had had his own nefarious appetites, and when Gregory, repulsed and full of disgust at the discovery, had brought this to their father's attention, he'd learned how little valued he was. A hard lesson but it had stood him in good stead since then. Now his entire family was dead and Gregory wasn't sure whether to grieve or exult.

England had changed since Gregory had last set foot there. His father had served as a knight and baronet under Edward III. There had been no distance Gregory could travel in the early days of his career as a sword for hire, that was far enough for England to be unheard of and respected as a military power. That respect had faded as the old king's health had failed. Then, four years ago, the king's grandson, ten-year-old Richard, had been crowned king on Edward's death. It was little surprise that a mere boy might have difficulty emerging from Edward's shadow. He'd ruled for five decades and was noted for his military success, having turned England into a formidable martial power. Little was heard from the boy-king, who had no single regent, but was advised by a series of councils made up of the most powerful and influential men of the realm. Gregory found it hard to feel the allegiance he ought to feel towards an untried child, who had yet to add any deeds of note to his name.

The sun was low on the horizon, casting Maudesley Castle as a stark black shape on the brow of the hill. Gregory reined Drum in on the edge of the village, unnerved by how quiet it was. He'd been riding through Maudesley lands for the last few hours. The neglected fields and overgrown roads told their tale of mismanagement, deepening the lines between Gregory's brows. The standing remains of a late and desperate harvest reminded him that a sickness had swept through his father's lands. Looking at the seemingly deserted village, the complete absence of smoke coming from the cott smoke holes, Gregory wondered if he was now lord of an estate peopled only by ghosts. An unwelcome thought which he couldn't entirely dismiss. He rode on.

Fletcher had been steward of Maudesley Castle since Gregory's father was a boy. Gregory remembered the shrewd, wiry, old man from his own childhood. Fletcher had already been well into middle years by then, but he was as hale as an oak, and still sharp witted. Both Gregory and William had learned the rudiments of maintaining an estate from Fletcher, the one area of their education where Gregory was the superior of the pair. Or at least, the more inclined to apply. Gregory had not considered that Fletcher might have died, and he should have done. After all, the man must be into his seventh decade, and the very old and very young were the favourite prey of sicknesses like the fever which had swept through Essex last year.

As Fletcher stood before him now, Gregory almost felt that the past eight years – the past two decades even – did not intervene. That he was a boy again and Fletcher had time to scold or teach him, or very occasionally praise him, where his father did not. Then Fletcher bowed stiffly, dipping his head, hair sparse and completely white. The illusion shattered. Gregory's father and brother, most of the village and fully half the servants were dead. Others had gone to find better paid work elsewhere.

"My lord," Fletcher murmured, equal parts relief and respect. "I'm glad you're home."

Gregory had been glad enough to leave Wynnstree, though the intervening years had not leached the bitterness from the memory. There was no chance of his father ever approving of him now. And even the most casual glance told him that getting Maudesley Castle and surrounding lands back in some sort of order – let alone making them profitable – would be no mean feat.

"It's good to see you, Fletcher."

Fletcher straightened painfully. "This is a sad homecoming, I fear."

Gregory's mouth pulled into something too grim to be a smile. "Don't give me a character I don't deserve, Fletcher. My family has been dead to me these past eight years. We've all only just agreed on the fact." A hint of vicious mirth entered his tone. "We were bound to agree upon something eventually."

Fletcher made a noise might have been a laugh before turning it into a cough. "I've had a chamber prepared for you, my lord."

He turned to leave but Gregory caught his arm. "Fletcher, what happened here? Not just the sickness. The castle...the fields..." The town. The population. The abandoned harvest. The broken gates and starved looking animals. The neglect of

8

the whole pox ridden estate.

Fletcher's gaze was hard. "That's a longer tale than I can yet give tongue to, my lord. It will go easier with ale and in any case, is best not swallowed on an empty stomach."

Gregory bit back further impatient questions and deferred to his steward's judgement.

3.

26th May, 1381

Gregory despaired of ever catching the thieves as he tracked them across Essex. They appeared to know the countryside even better than he did, and kept off the roads. He was furious that he was wasting valuable time chasing the miserable bastards in the opposite direction to London, which was where he needed to be. And beneath his frustration, and the gruesome punishments he mentally devised for when he finally caught the thieves, not to mention the treacherous groom, Gregory was enraged with himself. He'd finally scraped the money together, taking a harpy to his bed no less, and he'd acted no better than William would have done. Couldn't pass a tavern without pissing against its wall. It wasn't the first time Gregory had drunk too much. It wouldn't be the last. But he'd never allowed himself to become so inebriated that it compromised a mission. It was his new wife's fault – that was the only explanation. Everything had been out of balance since that chit of a girl had walked through the gatehouse of Maudesley Castle.

The trail grew colder and Gregory's impotent rage increased. Sharp stabs in his side when he moved too quickly reminded him of his cracked ribs. The pain in his head settled to a constant dull ache, but his jaw had stiffened, and he knew bruises bloomed across his face. He hadn't been beaten unconscious since he was a squire. The copious amounts of ale might have softened him up, but the wound to his pride went far deeper than broken ribs. Gregory intended to take it out of the thieves' hides when he caught them. If he caught them. He was starting to think he must have passed them without knowing it. Or that they had veered west, instead of heading north out of Essex.

There had been fresh hoof prints, most probably left by the two amblers, but he didn't think the entire party was mounted.

Of course an ambler was more suited to rugged terrain and a swift, distance devouring trot over long periods of time than a courser. Drum had to be regularly rested, lacking the distance endurance of the smaller horses. Not to mention the smoother gait. For the first time, Gregory regretted not purchasing a riding horse. It had seemed an unnecessary expense when he was only riding to London, but it would appear that Fletcher had been right yet again.

He pressed on to Littlefolds, more out of stubbornness than any great hope that he might catch the thieves now. The small town had a strange air of tension. Drovers were herding goats and geese, smoke spiralled out of chimneys, the metallic ring of struck iron indicated a smithy, but none of it seemed entirely natural. Gregory dismounted so Drum could drink at a trough, frowning at a group of commons and villeins gathered around a spare, older man – probably the town reeve. He wondered why they were not all working in the fields as they should have been on a fine spring day, then realised the reeve was reading aloud from a letter.

"John Shep, sometime St Mary priest of York and now in Colchester, greeteth well John Nameless, John Miller, John Carter, and biddeth Piers Ploughman to go to his work, and chastise well Hobbe the Robber."

Gregory's frown deepened. What in God's name was that supposed to mean? It was hardly St Paul to the Corinthians. Even stranger was the frantic energy it seemed to impart to the crowd. There were angry cries of agreement and promises to 'do our duty as God prompts us'. A chill crept up Gregory's spine. Fletcher had said these were troubled times. Indeed, Gregory could hardly have failed to notice that the courtesy and deference due to his rank and consequence were delivered in a forced and often resentful manner.

A rumour had been circulating for some time now. That if the feared French invasion were to take place, the English lords would find their own common folk siding with the invaders against them. Gregory had always dismissed it as unfounded suspicion. The commons had a fairly miserable lot. They chafed at restrictions put on what they could earn and buy and wear, on where they could sell their goods and how much they had to give up as tithes. On needing permission before their daughters could marry. Not to mention the resentment caused by bishops and priors insisting on their tenants using the mills owned by their estates, and charging those tenants through the nose to do so. But for all that, Gregory had always been confident that English common folk and villeins would side with English lords when it came down to it. Perhaps those who believed the Great Rumour were on to something after all.

"Are you looking for the smithy?" A cheerful voice broke in on Gregory's musings. "That's a lovely horse, you've got there."

Gregory discovered the speaker to be a scrawny, underfed and filthy boy, whose optimistic expression was at odds with his ragged cloths and bruised face. "No," Gregory was startled into replying. "I'm looking for a scarred man." He drew a line across his own cheek with a forefinger.

The boy had pale, slightly protuberant eyes that gave him a gormless look under a matted tangle of hair, so Gregory didn't really expect an intelligent answer.

"Yeah, I seen him. And his cronies. They spent a whole silver piece in the inn!" The boy's eyes bulged even further at this salacious piece of gossip. "More than they spent here any other time."

"They've been here before?" Gregory found he was gripping the boy's stick thin arm and loosened his fingers.

"Think the one with the scar had family here once. Turdman, he's called."

"Which way did they go?"

The boy shrugged. "Into the forest."

Gregory groaned internally. It would be dark in a couple of hours. He had no hope of catching them in strange woods on another lord's lands.

The boy eyed Gregory speculatively. "I reckon they won't go far though. They'll camp near the ford at Negethille."

Gregory leaned over the boy. "Where is this ford?"

The boy grinned, showing a mouthful of erupting incisors. "Can I pat your horse?"

***

The thieves had camped in a clearing near the ford, just as the ragged boy had said. Dusk fell and Gregory halted Drum far enough back in the trees to prevent alerting the party of brigands while he considered his options. It was four to one – Gregory had experienced worse odds. He was better armed, since his sword, dagger and armour had been locked in *The Crossed Keys'* storeroom before he began his drinking binge – apparently the innkeeper hadn't been completely stupid. Drum was as good as squad in his own right, despite his advancing years, and the rogues were unlikely to have Gregory's skill at combat. The thieves had advantages too however.

The head injury made Gregory's reactions slower and the cracked ribs were a problem. His right knee was painful too but it would bear his weight, so he ignored it. The more pressing issue was that numbers were not on his side. Having located the brigands, Gregory knew he could apply to the local *mesne* lord for aid. He might even thank Gregory for the chance to clear out a nest of outlaws. But it would take time. This did not appear to be a permanent base, even if the boy said he'd seen the men before. There was little to no chance the thieves would stay beyond a single night. Besides, Gregory could not afford his stolen property falling into the hands of someone who would not return it to him. The nobility were supposed to have been appointed to their position by God, but long experience had convinced Gregory there was nothing especially noble about his own class, nor that God, if he existed, had much to do with the matter.

As desirable as a party of armed men under his command might be, Gregory knew it would only take someone coughing or loosing an arrow prematurely, and the thieves would be off into the undergrowth through land they clearly knew better than their pursuers, taking his coin with them. Better to keep it simple. Himself, his horse, surprise. He would make it fast and brutal, and if any of them died, it was up to them whether they were on speaking terms with their maker.

Gregory waited in the growing darkness. Drum was restless but silent, sensing an oncoming battle. The thieves had felt confident enough to light a fire, which flickered bright between the trees. Gregory smelled roasting rabbit and clenched his teeth, hunger and rage fighting for dominance in his gut. Laughter and presumably ribald conversation drifted to him on the breeze, though distance robbed it of sense. His mind supplied meaning. How they congratulated themselves on a good haul. How they laughed at the stupid, drunk prick, who was such easy pickings when he staggered out of the inn for a piss. Gregory's jaw ached and his hands curled into fists.

He let them start in on their meal. Let them down a decent amount of whatever was in the skins they carried, before making his move. He mounted Drum and had the horse pick a slow, careful trail along the edge of the clearing, hoping any noises would be covered by the thieves' well lubricated laughter, or at least that it would be taken for a harmless creature such as a deer. One of the stolen amblers Gregory had used as a pack horse, lifted her head and snorted, before whickering loudly. The thieves paid no attention.

Gregory held Drum in position, feeling the tense anticipation of the horse's muscles. Drum knew better than to stamp or paw at the ground this close to action but every line of his body communicated his desire to charge. *You still think you're a youngster, my lad*, Gregory thought in grim amusement, silently drawing his sword. Just as the sound of laughter from the camp reached raucous proportions, Gregory touched his heels lightly to Drum's sides and the warhorse surged forwards. He bellowed wordlessly, brandishing his sword. Drum strung his neck out, picking up speed. Two of the men leapt to their feet in fright. Gregory rode down one of the men as he fumbled for a blade, whilst slashing the other across the chest. Blood sprayed, a glittering black arc in the firelight. The two slower thieves gained their feet. Gregory noted the scarred face of the nearer man and a fragment of memory sent his fury to new heights. The image of a club coming down on his ribs as he lay in the mud, blearily trying to fend it off with his naked hands. The scarred and grinning face of the club's wielder.

Gregory felt no great inclination to mercy.

The scarred man screamed and leapt back just as Gregory's sword parted the air where his head had been a moment before. It wasn't a totally wasted blow; the sword took his hand on the down stroke and it fell with a soft thud to land beside the fire. The man stumbled back, curled around the injury before falling to his knees. Gregory turned his attention to the last thief, confident the scarred man would neither die nor escape before he was finished with him. He recognised the treacherous groom and smiled.

The groom let out a whimper and fled. Drum whinnied and streamed after his prey without Gregory so much as twitching the reins. Sense began to permeate Gregory's lust for retribution. They were away from the light of the fire, the forest closed in dark and forbidding. Somewhere ahead was the ford. Drum took a fallen tree in a fluid leap and Gregory, now nearly blind after losing his night vision to the fire, had hard work to keep his seat. He brought the courser under control, slowing him to a trot. Drum fought the rein, not yet ready to give up the chase. Gregory pulled him to a halt, cursing under his breath at having lost the last thief.

A sharp crack on his left was all the warning he was given as a shape lunged out of the gloom. The false groom, cornered by thicket on one side and the nearby ford on the other, had decided on a desperate gambit. There wasn't enough light to gleam on the edge of the wickedly long knife as he raised it, but Gregory felt the weapon's presence through some half understood instinct and kicked out savagely. The thief swore and lunged again. He kept tight to Drum's left side, calculating that it was too enclosed for the knight to turn his horse or swing his sword easily.

Horses don't generally like to walk backwards, but Gregory had taught Drum far stranger tricks. Responding to the knight's muttered command, Drum trotted smartly back a few steps, spotted the thief who was now in biting range, and struck, quick as a striking snake. The courser's teeth closed on the meat of man's shoulder with a hideous crunch. The groom screamed, dropping the knife and falling on his arse when Drum made another lunge at him.

Gregory dismounted and collected the dropped knife. "Master Joiner, my loyal groom. You do remember me, I trust?"

Joiner made an unintelligible, blubbery noise.

Gregory patted Drum's neck, inspecting the knife. "Decent blade, this."

More phlegm choked mutterings littered the air.

"You were with hardened outlaws, Master Joiner. We're judged by the company we keep," Gregory said conversationally. "Don't move." He tapped the knife point below Joiner's eye for emphasis. "I make mistakes when I'm rushed."

Joiner shook. Shock and blood loss.

Gregory wasn't a great enthusiast of torture. He'd found that, properly motivated by fear, most men would tell him what he wanted to know, without resorting to peeling off their skins or burning out eyes. He'd left two men dead back at the camp, and the scarred man wouldn't be good for much either. The traitor groom was completely in his power and it was the money that was important. If they'd hidden it somewhere, he needed someone to question.

"What do you suppose the penalty for attacking and robbing a lord on his own lands is?" Gregory tightened his hold on Drum's reins. The big courser had a slightly too lively interest in the trembling thief.

"Please, milord. Times is hard and…" Joiner trailed off at the look on Gregory's face.

"I suggest you answer my next question as if your life depends on it."

Joiner inhaled sharply through his noise, a bubbling sound full of snot.

Gregory leaned in, knife pressed against Joiner's cheek. "Where. Is. My. Money?"

"T-Turdman," Joiner gasped.

"The ill-favoured fellow with the scar?"

"He's got it. Held on to all of it. Said we couldn't divide the spoils yet." Joiner added bitterly, "Was told not to trust Turdman One-hand. Should've never listened to him. Attacking a lord!"

"*One-hand*?" A horrible suspicion gripped Gregory. He thrust Joiner into a march in front of him and tugged on Drum's reins.

They returned to the overturned camp, where the fire still crackled merrily. Very little time had passed but there was no sign of the scarred man. Gregory knocked Joiner to his knees with a barked "Stay down!" Then he bent and picked up the hand he'd hacked from Turdman's wrist. Except it wasn't a hand, it was a glove stuffed with straw. Turdman had evidently lost a hand to thieving before. Such a marker would have made honest folk avoid him or treat him with suspicion, but he'd been clever enough to devise a decoy hand. Cunning enough to let Gregory think he'd seriously injured the bastard too, in order to make his escape. Turdman was gone, and Gregory's money with him.

Gregory turned a murderous glare on Joiner. The false groom had no intention of staying to be scapegoat to the knight's rage. He reached into the fire and flung a burning branch at Gregory's head. The knight ducked and made a grab for Joiner, but the thief had threw himself towards the amblers. Gregory might still have caught him, if his foot hadn't slid on one of the scattered firestones, forcing his weight on to his injured knee, which buckled. He went down hard, the pain in his knee and ribs flaring briefly into agony. By then the groom had scrambled on the back of one of the horses and was urging it into a full gallop from a standing start.

Joiner's success was short lived. He wasn't quite beyond the reach of the firelight when a low branch swept him off the saddle. The frantic horse crashed onward into the dark, indifferent to its fallen rider. Gregory took a burning branch from the fire and went to the crumpled heap. Joiner's head was caved in on one side and blood oozed sluggishly down his face. He was dead.

"Bollocks in hell." Gregory stamped back towards the fire,

checking the picket on the other ambler while he was at it. The mare was restive and rolled her eyes at his approach, but she wouldn't be going anywhere.

Drum snorted, edging sideways, not especially keen on being picketed with the remaining ambler. If Gregory had been a fanciful man he might have attributed his warhorse with an 'I told you so' air.

"I know, I should have just let you bite his face off and had done with it," he muttered soothingly. Inside, Gregory was once again equal parts fury and frustration. The thieves were dead or gone and he was no closer to recovering his money.

A dark patch gleamed wetly next to the fire. Gregory brought the burning branch closer. Blood. Right where the decoy hand had fallen. Had he managed to cut Turdman? He cast a surreptitious glance around the clearing and his gaze latched on a large oak nearby. Perhaps all wasn't lost after all.

Gregory tossed the burning branch back into the fire. He went through the tasks of removing Drum's saddle and bridle, and rubbing him down. You always took care of your horse first and he'd never been one to leave that to an ostler or squire. Not that he'd ever had a squire. Or even a personal groom, unless you counted Joiner. If that experience was anything to go by, he'd do without. Gregory dragged the corpses further off in to the woods for wolves or lynxes to fight over, if they cared to. Waste not want not.

He wrapped his cloak around himself, sinking on to a log and pulling the stopper from one of the thieves' wineskins. It turned out to be decent stuff, probably stolen or purchased with stolen coin. The rabbit was slightly too well done but tasted ambrosial when seasoned with hunger. To an outside observer, he appeared to be a man settling himself down for the night. Disappointed not to have recovered his money, but reconciled to it being gone. Gregory appeared to stare at the flames, letting his head nod. In truth, he looked into the darkness with half closed eyes, and waited.

Gregory had both received and dealt violence for much of his life. He'd never developed an appetite for killing for its own sake though, any more than he took pleasure in using violence to dominate an opponent much weaker than himself. He might cuff a lazy farm hand or throw a cup of wine at an annoying servant. If Gregory had ever acquired the courtesy and pretty manners of a knight, he'd lost them together with his shining ideals. Being a mercenary had encouraged a more practical mindset. It had never mattered that he was thought uncouth, he was no a courtier after all. Violence was a necessary tool, and Gregory was at peace with that.

But there were those of the so-called nobility who thought it their God-given right to beat and bully their inferiors for fun. Like William, when he realised no one would stop the golden son of Baronet Maudesley. That same breed of noble stock, Gregory had observed, were often the kind who refused an honest fight. You wouldn't see them in the lists at a tourney. In war, they were exceptionally good at leading from the back. Let his common folk think he was foul tempered. Let his servants creep in fear of him. Let his wife believe he was an unmannerly brute. What did it signify? Better that than to be an over dressed, simpering codpiece who beat servants and ran away from battle.

The fire died down to a bank of red coals. The shadows lengthened. He heard a faint noise on his sinister side, the shifting of weight perhaps. The break and fall of a twig from its bough and the faint sound it made as it hit the forest floor. He grinned savagely. Why cut down the tree when with a little patience the apple would fall at your feet?

4.

20th March, 1381
Twelve Weeks Earlier

Fletcher suggested that Gregory might solve his financial problems through marriage. This was after his steward had softened him up by appraising him of the true state of the Maudesley lands.

"Your father, God rest his soul, had long trusted William with many matters concerning the running of the estate and its farms." Fletcher hesitated as if unwilling to speak ill of Gregory's brother.

"You may as well speak plainly. I know exactly what William was." Gregory groped blindly for his ale. Fletcher nudged the mug towards Gregory's outstretched hand.

"If you ask for much plainness of speech, I fear I will offend you, my lord," Fletcher warned.

Gregory took a swig from his mug, setting it down with a thud. He swiped foam from his whiskers with the back of his wrist. "Fletcher, get to the point. What did William do? Empty the strong room pursuing whores and dice?"

"If that were all, we might have weathered the last eight years better than we have." Fletcher eyed Gregory shrewdly. For all his deference and respect, he wasn't intimidated by his liege. "Your brother spent money as if he was minting it himself. He had a taste for fine clothes and jewels – you remember?" Gregory nodded and Fletcher went on. "Maudesley is not one of the truly wealthy estates, as you know, my lord."

Gregory grunted, impatient with Fletcher for stringing this out. But he did know. The Maudesley lands did not encompass any quarries or mines; they did not produce salt or silver; there were no great tracts of forest for timber; its towns and villages were small and had correspondingly small fairs. Trade had always been good but never met the excellence of that found in the larger, more varied towns. Maudesley wealth, such as it was, came almost exclusively from farming. It occurred to Gregory that Fletcher was laying it out piece by piece to ensure that he understood the full scope of the problem.

"Even so," Fletcher continued, "we might have continued in the way we always had before. Your brother spent the reserves of coin and liquidated many of the precious items for spending money, but we had the harvests, the flocks and herds. Lord William had us living hand to mouth, but we *were* living."

Gregory's heavy brows pulled inward, his jaw hardening. "Hand to mouth is only a step away from beggary. It wants only one disaster."

"Quite so, my lord. And we had several." Fletcher ticked them off on his fingers. "There was a murrain in the sheep and it spread to the cattle. We lost half our flocks and herds, at a conservative estimate."

So there had been little or no money earned from wool or dairy, then. "Go on."

"Then there was a blight in the crops. We've always grown half wheat, half rye. A mistake, as it turns out," Fletcher said flatly. "The rye was poisoned and poisoned all who tried to eat it. And some did, for they were hungry enough. By that point, I had hard enough work to have the crops burned in the fields, because a sickness had spread unchecked through the town, and then the other settlements."

Fletcher's voice faded in and out as Gregory tried to make sense of it all. Words like 'fever', 'purging', 'death toll' drifted to the surface in a senseless stew of noise and misery. He had inherited his father's lands only to find that those same lands were a drain not a boon. A worthless inheritance for the least valued son. Fitting, no?

"No one knows when Master William began borrowing money against a future turn in the estate's fortunes," Fletcher said, bringing Gregory abruptly back to the moment.

Gregory threw back his head and laughed. Worthless. It was all worthless. Had he thought something of value would come to him from his estranged family after all this time? Had he thought to be valued in his turn? Fletcher leant away from him at the deranged sound, eyes widening beneath his thick, white eyebrows. Fury burned through the demented humour. Gregory slammed his fist down on the table hard enough to make the ale jug and plates dance along the surface.

"And just what did you do to check this state of affairs?" He demanded, thrusting a finger towards Fletcher's chest. "Where was your counsel? Your wisdom? Where was your careful management? God's Blood, I've been buggered up the arse by a degenerate and an old fool, and you've acted as panderer for them!"

Fletcher didn't quail at Gregory's fury, merely regarded him with weary resignation. Infuriated, Gregory thrust his chair back and began to pace. Anything to alleviate this sudden, impotent need for action. For retribution.

"I did what I could, my lord," Fletcher said.

Gregory picked up the ale jug and hurled it at the wall, following it with his own mug. The jug, plain earthenware, exploded in a shower of dark liquid and paler shards of pottery. The mug was metal and merely hit the stone with a muted clang. Gregory watched the loam-dark drops drip down the wall, breathing heavily. His fists kept working themselves open and closed. There was a distant stab of chagrin at his loss of control and he strove to master himself.

"My advice...my pleas, were not heeded, my lord," Fletcher said calmly. "But I don't excuse myself. It was my failing that brought us to this. If I'd schooled your brother in his duties better..."

He let the sentence taper off but Gregory had the curious certainty that while Fletcher's words were sincere, his whole method of presentation was for effect. He sat back down in his chair and met Fletcher's gaze.

"That was unworthy of me," he murmured – as close to an apology as he would ever venture. "And you need not trouble yourself to claim my brother's faults. William was a man and subject to none save God." Gregory snorted. "You can gild a dog turd but it's still a turd."

Fletcher cleared his throat, smoothing away what looked

suspiciously like the start of a smile with one gnarled hand.

"Are they all dead?" Gregory said. "The townsfolk? The villeins?"

"Many of them. The others…" Fletcher grimaced. "The others went where the work is paid better. Or paid at all."

"Miserable traitors," Gregory said, without heat. He wouldn't expect a free man or woman to stay and work without wages. And he wouldn't have trusted their intentions if they did.

"Sickness has a way of making even the brave and loyal prey to strange fears." Fletcher was old enough to remember when the Black Pestilence had swept through England like the Angel of Death. "I managed to retain the core household but there was little I could do about the others. Your father had a few blood bondsmen but many were killed by the fever."

"And the fever is truly gone?"

"Yes, my lord. Your father and brother were among the last to succumb."

Gregory said nothing for a moment, then laughed grimly. "Sickness. Poor harvests. Pestilence in the flocks. Death and abandonment by the common folk. No plague of locusts? No storms of hail and fire?"

"My lord?"

"It would seem my brother offended God. I was speculating on what else I could expect."

"There is the matter of *Primer Seisin*, my lord." At Gregory's look of incomprehension, Fletcher explained. "Upon your father and brother's death, all Maudesley lands reverted to the possession of the *mesne* lord. Who also died of the fever and has not yet been replaced. Law in Lexden is scarcely any better than in Wynnstree. Both estates reverted to the crown. King Richard is now the mesne lord."

This struck Gregory harder than any news he had yet heard. These weren't even his lands. As ill-tended, neglected and mismanaged as they were, he'd still thought this estate, this castle, was his. But of course they were not. His father and brother had died over a year ago. Even if Gregory had been here to inherit directly, the king would still have had to confirm him as heir. Oaths had to be sworn.

And Gregory had not been here. The Maudesley lands had been in contention for a year.

"I have to pay homage to the king," Gregory said.

"You'll need to do more than that," Fletcher said. "You'll need to prove you're the true heir, which should be simple enough. The real problem is the inheritance fee."

Gregory's gut knotted. "How much?"

"One year's full profits of the Maudesley estate. Though, as the inheritance is under dispute, the king's treasurer might be generous and only ask for half a year's worth." Fletcher's tone said he did not think this was especially likely.

"A year's profits?" Gregory exploded. "What profits?"

"That would be the dilemma, my lord." He rose slowly and went to pick up the pieces of the smashed ale jug. "I don't suppose you amassed a large fortune on your travels?"

Gregory glared at the old man's bent back. "I cannot raise money on the land until I own the land. And I cannot own the land until the king confirms me as heir, which he will not do unless I pay him money raised on one year's working of the land."

"Makes the whole situation appear somewhat dire," Fletcher commented unhelpfully.

"What was my brother intending to do?" Gregory demanded. "When he wasn't pissing all the profits and most of the strong room contents up a wall, how did he intend to inherit?" He didn't really expect an answer. 'What would William do?' was a question calculated to get you stuck in the midden not out of it.

Fletcher raised his head. "When your father fell sick, he started looking around for suitable wealthy brides. Not that he got far since he was taken by the fever himself soon after."

"Marriage?" Gregory said with distaste.

Fletcher shrugged. "You'll need to sooner or later, my lord. If you intend to continue the Maudesley name."

"What high born maiden marries this?" Gregory swept an arm out in a gesture that might have indicated the neglected castle, the unworked lands or his own scarred and unlovely person. "Any virtuous, well-bred woman with the sort of wealth I need, would have her pick of far more tempting suitors."

Fletcher gave Gregory a look that in a younger man might have been considered mischievous. "I may have a candidate for you, my lord. Well-born, wealthy. Beddable enough, too, I imagine. If you're willing to be less picky about where she's from and her virtue, she could well be the solution to our problem."

Gregory did not like the glint in his steward's eye but another hour of chasing their tails for alternative solutions proved fruitless. He agreed to at least meet the girl's guardian. In his heart, Gregory knew that short of finding his bride in a brothel, if her dowry was large enough, the deed was as good as done.

5.

26th May, 1381

The splash of blood Gregory had found beside the stuffed glove had long since dried in the heat of the fire. The faint glow of the embers did little to penetrate the shadows. High above, in the branches of the oak, whose trunk also bore smears of dried blood, a lumpen piece of darkness detached itself from the whole to slowly creep down to the forest floor. A night bird trilled, followed by the distant, doleful hoot of an owl. Several times the lump of darkness paused in its descent, shaking with effort, to listen for any unusual sounds. But even the great warhorse was drowsing on its feet on the far side of the fire.

As the shape attempted to negotiate the final few feet, the sharp yipping cry of a fox tore through the night. The shape swore and swiped at a hand hold. It missed and landed in a breathless heap at the base of the tree.

Gregory loomed out of the dark and smiled down at the scarred man. "A good evening to you. Master Turdman, isn't it?"

"Ah...ah..." Turdman wheezed, kicking his legs in a futile attempt to rise.

Gregory rested a large, sabaton clad foot on his chest. "Don't get up on my account."

"I can explain," Turdman said.

"I'm not interested in why you did it," Gregory said. "I'm not even in the mood to turn your miserable hide into a new saddlebag for damn near killing me with that club – inventive idea to lash it to the stump of a lost hand, by the way." He allowed some of his weight to transfer to Turdman's chest and throat. The scarred man thrashed, foam appearing on his lips as he fought for air. His good hand and the severed stump beat a useless tattoo against Gregory's chausses covered calf.

Gregory eased up and Turdman coughed violently. He waited with the terrible patience of a hunter that knows his prey is almost run to the end of its strength. When he was certain he had the scarred man's full attention again, he spoke. "Where is my money?"

"Here! H-here! I buried it."

"Show me." Gregory hauled Turdman to his feet, clamping a large, gauntleted hand on the nape of his neck. Turdman whimpered but the fight had left him. He was injured and exhausted. Gregory knew he was hoping for a moment's distraction in which he could run. Turdman led him a few paces back into the trees, where a hollow at the base of a beech had been partially filled in with leaves and loam. He uncovered the saddlebags, showing Gregory the glinting coins inside.

"Did you spend any of it?"

"A few coins." Turdman swallowed, adding somewhat bitterly, "There wasn't time for more."

"This will be quick then." Gregory grabbed Turdman's neck again.

"Wait!" Turdman wriggled in a futile attempt to get away.

"Yes?" Gregory said.

"You can't kill me!"

"Can I not?" Gregory said.

"Please!" Bubbles of snot and spit mingled on Turdman's face.

"So you can attack someone who can't track you down?" Gregory glanced at the severed stump of Turdman's left hand. The scarred man had already had two chances. Gregory set his other hand just below Turdman's jaw. In one swift motion, he pulled up and twisted the thief's head sideways. There was a sharp crack as Turdman's neck broke, followed by a thud as Gregory dropped him. The scarred man gazed up, eyes bulging and sightless over his crushed throat.

"I promised it would be quick."

***

Gregory set off before dawn, intending to bypass the town of Littlefolds entirely as he regained the road to London. He'd lost enough time chasing the thieves north, then having to double back. However, as the sun touched the crest of the hill, Drum threw a shoe. Muttering profanities, Gregory dismounted and examined the horse's foot. No injury. Perhaps the night time charge through the forest glade had loosened the shoe. More expense. More delay. Full of frustration, Gregory took Drum's reins in one hand and began to walk the courser towards the distant church steeple as the sun limned it in early morning light. The ambler he'd reclaimed from the thieves trotted placidly after them.

The atmosphere in town was even more charged than the day before, or perhaps it was more noticeable because he walked amongst them on foot. Snatches of conversation came to Gregory's ears – mostly centred on the likely visit of a tax collector from London. From the bits and pieces he made out, the general air of discontent was over the poll tax – a flat rate fee levied on every viable individual, which took no account of personal circumstances. Gregory found, to his surprise, that he had some sympathy with the discontented townsfolk. Was he not in a very similar position with his inheritance fee? The circumstances and misfortunes of his own estate were not being considered. It was sobering to discover that his own concerns were not so different from those of the commons.

Aside from bitter complaints about unfair taxation, and mutterings about assaults on unmarried daughters, a name kept cropping up. John Ball. Gregory had never heard of the cleric, which wasn't surprising since he'd only been back in England a few months. It sounded as if the man had said things that caught the imagination of the commons. Which made him a potentially dangerous man. Gregory knew that the sort of energy now moving through the lower echelons of society could break out in terrifying violence with the right provocation. There was no reasoning with hungry masses, nor with those who believed they had been unjustly treated and that God was on their side.

"You're back!" A voice cried. "Did you find 'em? Did you give 'em a good thrashing?"

Gregory had reached the smithy. He recognised the boy who'd given him the thieves' whereabouts. Not a goose-boy or a stable lad after all, but a blacksmith's apprentice. Gregory's mouth tightened as he regarded the boy. Pursuit of the thieves had made Gregory inattentive yesterday but the bright morning light left no illusions. The boy was even scrawnier than he'd realised. A mere scrap of humanity, filthy with soot and grime which was still insufficient to hide the mottled patterns of bruising on his skin. It ranged from almost healed yellow smudges to the deep blue-black of newly acquired marks. At a generous estimate, the boy was around twelve years old. He'd already had his nose broken at least twice. One skinny arm was slightly crooked as if it too had been broken and then set badly. A faint pink scar crossed the boy's forehead and divided an eyebrow.

Pain in his temples forced Gregory to unclench his jaw. The boy was clearly indentured. He shouldn't interfere. "Where is your master, boy?"

"Out the back. Did you get them thieves?"

"Just fetch your master," Gregory said.

"Alright, my lord." The boy hurried across the yard, pausing to call back over his shoulder, "You got a lovely horse, my lord. Where did you get the other one? Can you tell me about smashing up them thieves when I get back?"

He was gone before Gregory could reply, leaving the knight to look over the smithy. The yard was hard packed earth with a decent fence surrounding it and plenty of room for a horse. The tools, a glimpse of which could be seen through the open door of the forge proper, were clearly good quality. The place was neat and orderly. The boy's master was making a decent living for himself.

The blacksmith rounded the corner, with the boy limping painfully behind him, face white. Gregory told himself again that it was none of his business.

The blacksmith, meanwhile, did not seem impressed with his

customer. At least not until he took in the sight of Drum. It might be easy to mistake Gregory for someone of far lower social station than he was at first glance, but no one who knew horses would mistake Drum for anything other than what he was. The blacksmith's eyes twinkled in their rolls of flesh, roving over Gregory's sword, his cloak – no commoner was permitted to wear such an item, however threadbare – and finally rested on the full saddlebags carried by the ambler. He held out his broad, heat hardened hands and smiled obsequiously.

"My lord, how can I be of assistance?"

"My horse has thrown a shoe." Gregory didn't add that he was in a hurry. There was a law limiting how much a smith could charge for shoeing a horse but some found ways around it by adding a fee for fast work.

"Happy to assist, my lord, but I'm a busy man."

Gregory bit back a harsh retort and showed a flash of coin. "This needn't take too much of your time."

They fell to the business of haggling, finally settling on more than Gregory wanted to pay but less than the blacksmith asked. Drum heaved a horsey sigh, but complied with the muttered order to stand still. Gregory kept a tight hold on the reins, not liking the way Drum's eye rolled towards the blacksmith. Apparently the horse had taken as instant a dislike to the man as Gregory had himself.

The shoe was fitted, with the boy fetching and carrying at his master's behest. Gregory couldn't help noticing that no matter how the blacksmith cuffed and cursed him, nothing seemed to dent the boy's high spirits. He could see how that might grate after a while – servants were supposed to be useful but essentially invisible after all. Even so, Gregory disliked the heavy handed way the blacksmith dealt with the boy, especially since in all other respects he seemed to do his work well. He obviously wasn't lazy and seemed to have some quickness of wits. A lad with potential, in other words.

Leave it alone, he told himself. *You have enough to concern you.*

And then the blacksmith aimed a kick at the boy, who dodged

it instinctively but knocked a bucket of nails flying in the process. The blacksmith fell on him with a flurry of blows from a leather strap, cursing the useless, lazy, worthless... Gregory's hand flashed out, catching the man's arm as he drew it back for another blow.

The blacksmith was red faced, almost apoplectic with rage as he turned towards Gregory.

"You don't mean to kill the lad, surely?" Gregory said mildly. The blood thrummed through his veins in anticipation of violence. The feel of the blacksmith's arm in his grasp called vividly to mind that little twist and pull manoeuvre that was always rewarded with the satisfying crack of bone. No strength was required at all. The blacksmith's fierce expression frayed and, reluctantly, Gregory released his arm.

"Have you finished shoeing my horse? I have a distance to travel yet," Gregory said, distracting himself from his own violent inclinations. He noticed the boy had got himself well out of the way and was now trying to blend in with one of the soot stained walls. The lad was no fool, for all his eager to please ways and puppyish enthusiasm. Gregory gave Drum a final once over while the blacksmith waited with ill-concealed impatience for his money. *Don't do it*, he told himself. *Don't interfere.*

He knew he'd merely postponed the boy's beating for later, when there was no one to intervene. He knew also, that it didn't become a man of his station to take too much interest in another man's servants. The lightening of his purse as he paid the blacksmith, weighed on him. He would have bed and board to pay for in London, and stabling for Drum and the mare. He had no real need of a servant, especially not a half-starved boy. He thought of his wife's dowry, tucked safely in the saddlebags, not to be touched until it was signed over as his inheritance fee. And there was the time he had lost chasing after the thieves, and the fact that very countryside and all its folk felt like dry tinder – a casual spark would set England alight. Gregory wanted no part of that. The sooner he had reached London and sworn his oath of homage, the sooner he could be back in Wynnstree, repairing his lands and avoiding his wife.

A catalogue of good reasons not to interfere.

The boy gazed at Drum with admiration. The lad liked horses and was good with them. He was hardly big enough for a sparrow's supper. The ambler probably wouldn't even notice his weight added to the packs on its back. Gregory saw where that train of thought was leading and tried to rein himself in. He'd once believed in a code that endorsed protecting those weaker and less powerful than yourself. But that had been many years and many battles ago. That had been before William's nature ripened into something monstrous and no one had sought to check him, save Gregory. Only a fool believed in such a code after seeing the things Gregory had seen.

If the boy had shot a single look of pleading at Gregory, the knight might have hardened his heart against him. Instead, the lad's expression said he expected no more of life than this, and it was good enough.

"How much for the boy?" Gregory placed the last penny in the blacksmith's hand.

"Eh?" The Blacksmith blinked stupidly. "You mean Cuthbert?"

"He does have a name then," Gregory muttered. "How much?"

"My lord, you can't just come in and buy another man's servant. Meaning no disrespect."

Gregory fixed the blacksmith with a hard stare, using his height and physical presence to lour over him menacingly. The blacksmith wasn't a small man but he had nothing on the knight. He certainly wasn't a trained and battle hardened warrior. He shrank back, losing his proprietary manner.

"Can I not?" Gregory said softly. "How did you come by the lad? He's not your son and I cannot imagine he would work for you if he were free to find work elsewhere."

Anger and fear warred for dominance in the blacksmith's face. "His mother and father gave him into my keeping."

"They sold me to him to pay a debt," The boy...*Cuthbert* piped up.

"So you'll have his indenture papers," Gregory said. The blacksmith shifted his weight uneasily. "You boy, do you have your half of the papers?"

Cuthbert looked blank. "Didn't see no papers."

"The boy couldn't read them in any case," the blacksmith said. "It was an informal arrangement. His parents saw no need to make it official…"

Beads of sweat had formed at Gregory's hairline at the thought of having to read an official document here and now. He resisted the urge to swipe his brow. Let the blacksmith think it was the heat of the smithy.

"If money changed hands, it was official," Gregory said. "There should have been a writ of indenture. That boy's parents weren't selling a cow. They were allowing you to purchase an apprentice." He cast an unfavourable eye over Cuthbert again. "How long have you had him?"

"A y-year—"

"Two years, and half another," Cuthbert chirped, falling abruptly silent under the furious glare the blacksmith sent his way.

"A reasonable amount of time," Gregory mused. "How's he coming along with his horse shoes?"

"Er…"

"They must be complicated and thus require much study," Gregory went on. "Nails?"

The blacksmith wilted.

"So what has the lad learned under your tutelage, aside from how to dodge a kick?"

The blacksmith glared at Gregory who smiled chillingly back. If a lord wanted to buy a boy's indenture from a common man, there was little the latter could do but comply. A note of pleading entered the blacksmith's tone. "Why concern yourself with such things, my lord?"

"I've use for a lad to look after my horses and gear. Cuthbert looks like he'll do well enough," Gregory said. His smile was predatory. "A shilling as recompense for his apprenticeship."

"I paid three shillings for him and he's had three years of training since then!" The Blacksmith squawked, forgetting his earlier story.

"He paid eight pence for me, I was listening," Cuthbert said helpfully.

Gregory swallowed the sudden urge to laugh. It wasn't funny. God only knew what possessed him because no doubt he'd want to thrash the lad himself before he got to London. "A shilling's a fair exchange, then."

The satisfaction of thwarting the cheese-pale and furious blacksmith was so great, that Gregory didn't even feel the loss of the shilling.

6.

15th April, 1381
Six Weeks Earlier

Her name was Alienor Douglas and she was a March Lord's daughter. Held to be comely enough − by Borderland Scot's standards at least. As well as competent and accomplished, and more importantly, rich. Possessed of a substantial enough dowry at any rate. While you might never be able to tell who her family would support between one Sunday and the next, a connection with a powerful and wealthy Scottish lord was not to be disdained, no matter what more squeamish suitors might say. Furthermore, the lady was said to be good natured, if a little…tempestuous in her actions − nothing the careful guidance of a good husband couldn't correct. Alienor was also well educated and intelligent − a circumstance that led to an unfortunate tendency to speak her mind; in the presence of men even. But, the girl's guardian hastened on, she was surely a most suitable bride despite this.

Gregory listened to this list of his new beloved virtues wearing a stony expression. He remembered Baron de Gilbert from his boyhood. The man seemed to have aged twenty years in the last ten. Gregory recalled a robust, quick, stern man. De Gilbert had been his brother's master when William became a squire. He eyed the white haired man before him and thought he'd never seen the old patrician look so sheepish. The baron clearly knew he was offering shoddy goods to the son of a man who had once been his close friend.

De Gilbert was far too eager to sell. Whatever was wrong with this Alienor of the Marches, it had been enough to prevent any other matrimonial nibbles. It could simply be that no one else was quite desperate enough to marry a Scot. But coupled with the haste with which de Gilbert wanted to be rid of his niece,

Gregory had a strong suspicion he knew what the flaw in the gem was.

Fletcher had already given Gregory a brief overview of local rumour concerning Lady Alienor. Then, reluctantly, he'd given a far more detailed account. Much of it Gregory had dismissed as gossip, but there was a troubling thread of continuity to be followed. One that reminded him such rumours began somewhere.

In the face of Gregory's noticeable lack of enthusiasm, Baron de Gilbert trailed off.

"If the lady is half as attractive and accomplished as you say, I wonder that you've not suggested one of your own sons should marry her," Gregory said smoothly. "Lionel and Piers are already wed, I know. But Giles is still without a wife, is he not?"

The baron's pleasant expression stiffened. "Alienor is my sister's daughter, Sir Maudesley. Far too close a relation for the laws of consanguinity to permit. Besides, Giles is to take holy orders at Lammastide."

"My congratulations," Gregory said, not pointing out that becoming a priest or a monk did not stop a man from taking a wife. "Still, it does seem strange that the lady has not met with a suitable match, neither here nor in her father's lands."

The baron gave Gregory a long, measuring look. "You've already heard of my niece's indiscretion."

Gregory allowed the silence to stretch out taut and uncomfortable between them. He knew damn well he had to marry the girl but he wanted the truth first. And there was no reason for de Gilbert to think him eager, or more accurately, desperate.

"Alienor was sent here to learn the arts of running a household under my wife's guidance for a year or two. My brother-in-law allowed her to run somewhat wild, I think, though nothing was said at the time. And then…recently…she was found…with a man…"

"Not one she could marry, I take it." Gregory's tone was business-like but the words tasted sour.

"We don't know who the devil was," the baron said, with a flash of temper. "The wretched girl won't tell us."

"As long as he's not likely to turn up in a few months' time demanding his wife," Gregory said morosely. Damn Fletcher. The girl was a stale. He supposed from a practical point of view it didn't matter. Or it wouldn't matter if everyone in the surrounding area didn't already know.

"No, of course not," De Gilbert said hastily.

Gregory imagined being mocked by villein and lord alike for taking a soiled petticoat to wife. Not that there were that many people left on his own lands to laugh at him, but he supposed it required no great feats of mental agility to put those circumstances together and find something even greater to laugh at. The humbling of the Maudesley Baronetcy. A new thought struck him like a crossbow quarrel.

"And this haste to see the lady wed is due to fear of retribution from your powerful brother-in-law?" Gregory's jaw clenched. "Or that your niece's indiscretion will be compounded by an addition to the family in the near future?"

Baron de Gilbert met his gaze squarely. "Perhaps both. Does is matter, Maudesley?"

Gregory started at hearing his father's friend address him as if he were speaking to the old baronet.

De Gilbert's eyes grew hard. "As I understand matters, it has been several years of poor harvest for your estate. And with inheritance duty, I imagine you are in want of coin."

Gregory glowered at the older man, fists tightening on the arms of his chair.

The baron sat back and poured more ale into his mug. "My niece has a considerable dowry, for the right suitor. One of good family with the right name. I am prepared to be generous."

"How generous?" Gregory grated the words out past his locked teeth.

"Quite generous," De Gilbert said. "It would seem we might solve each other's problems admirably."

Gregory was glad the baron couldn't know of his brother's debts or doubtless 'quite generous' would have become 'slightly generous'. "We have an agreement then, providing your niece agrees."

A troubled expression crossed de Gibert's face before he

schooled it to a polite expression once more. "I'm sure she will see what a fine opportunity it is. She should have joined us by now." He rose from his chair. Gregory stood likewise but the baron waved him back into his seat. "No, no. I'll just…see what's keeping her."

He shut the door so firmly that it bounced partway open again and stood ajar, leaving Gregory to wonder why a man with a perfectly functioning household should feel compelled to go and fetch his wayward niece himself.

The question was answered in part some minutes later, when the sound of a hasty patter of footsteps accompanied by a heavier tread came from the corridor.

"I see I have no choice but to meet him," a young woman's voice said bitterly. "But I will promise no more than that."

Gregory knew it was ill done to eavesdrop but the woman's voice caught his attention. It softened words, rolling 'R's, lengthening 'L's and broadening vowels as it lilted up and down. It took him a moment to understand the words. His ear was not trained for a March accent, which was more than halfway to lowland Scottish.

"Alienor, in the name of God, you must see reason. Eligible suitors do not merely drop out of the sky," Baron de Gilbert said, in exasperation.

"Apparently this one has. Perhaps if you call on the Almighty again, He'll send a few more." There was disdain in every syllable. "Much good it may do you if He does, for I'll not agree to marry any of them."

"Alienor–"

"It's bad enough you'll not credit me with telling the truth, but you'd have me take as my husband any man who can bear arms!" There was a rhythmic pattern of steps and a faint swishing noise. To and fro. Back and forth. Lady Alienor was pacing in the corridor. "William Maudesley was a brute and I've heard nothing to say the brother is any better!"

Gregory stopped pretending that he wasn't listening with great interest.

"You've heard nothing of him at all," de Gilbert said, sounding as if he had run to the end of his patience. "He's been away from home almost ten years. There cannot be a score of people left alive who even remember him. See sense, Niece, I pray you."

There was a moment's unbroken silence.

"You cannot stay here forever," de Gilbert went on. "Your father expects you to marry from here or to return home and find a husband there. Your indiscretion—"

"It's as much to your advantage as to mine that Laird Douglas hears nothing of my indiscretion, as you call it."

"That's as maybe, but how long do you suppose it will be before word does reach his ears? You may dislike my methods, Niece, but how do they compare to your father's? Laird Douglas is a proud man, is he not?"

A pause as the lady considered the implication of these words. "Very well. I suppose you'd better present me to this 'suitable candidate'."

The door swung open and Gregory turned to see a tall, dark haired, young woman stride through it. He thought she was about nineteen – a comfort since he had no desire to marry a child. He rose and bowed, straightening to see chagrin pink her cheeks as she dipped a bow in return. She wasn't completely immune to propriety then, for all that she was from the Marches and had besmirched her virtue.

Gregory supposed she was pleasant enough to gaze upon. Rather lovely, in fact. He found himself the subject of her cool, assessing gaze and heat climbed the back of his neck, knowing what she saw. Or rather what she didn't see, since he conspicuously lacked any sign of great wealth, refinement or personal attraction. If the lady hoped for a true hearted knight from a ballad, she was likely to be disappointed. Not that it should matter. She should be grateful he was making an offer. From the still, cold expression she wore, he didn't think that gratitude would be forthcoming anytime soon.

Fletcher had cautioned him on how to address a delicately reared, young maiden, but he couldn't imagine honeyed words winning the day here. If the girl was beautiful, it was the sort of beauty a kestrel might possess – one not easily tamed or caged, and always entirely predatory.

"My niece, Alienor," de Gilbert said to Gregory, somewhat redundantly. "Alienor, my dear, this is Sir Gregory Maudesley…Baronet Maudesley now, I should say."

"Lady," Gregory dipped his head slightly, not seeing the point in bowing again when he'd just done so.

"My lord," Alienor said. "I would like to say it is a pleasure but you'll find me distressingly honest in all things." She shot a glance at her guardian, who shut his eyes and supressed a groan. Her gaze returned to Gregory's, full of undeclared challenge.

"Alienor," de Gilbert hissed through his teeth.

"All's well, my lord." Gregory was completely freed from his previous embarrassment, at liberty to speak his mind now that the lady had been so thoroughly rude. "I don't especially require sweet words from a wife. If I want a woman to talk in such a manner, I'll pay a professional."

"Maudesley!" de Gilbert snapped.

Gregory watched Alienor's expression. She didn't blush or pale. The only change was that the little frown scribbled between her fine, dark brows eased as they rose in surprise. The corner of her mouth twitched and for a moment Gregory could have sworn she wanted to laugh. If he had expected to embarrass her or shame her into silence, it hadn't worked.

"What *do* you require from a wife, then, if I may be so bold?" Alienor said.

Once again, Gregory was caught by the lilting quality of her voice that concealed the sharp edges of her words like hidden blades. "What any man requires of a wife." Seeing that answer did not satisfy her, he expanded on the subject. "A well run household, children if God wills it. The usual things."

Alienor smiled, the expression so sweet and deadly, Gregory fought not to step back. "And does it trouble you that you would not be marrying a virtuous, young maiden but one who has stained her reputation? That's a thorn to the pride, isn't it?"

"Yes," Gregory said, thinking there was no point dissembling. "But not enough to deter me."

Alienor's eyebrows lifted again.

"It need not be an insurmountable barrier," he went on, fumbling for words that were true even if he did find it

40

distasteful.

Alienor's expression was equal parts scorn and curiosity. "I believe you mean that."

"I'll not have any lovers turning up on my lands, mind. Past or future."

"Oh you've made your position very clear," Alienor's tone dripped more of that deadly sweetness.

Gregory wondered if this might not be a huge mistake. She was strongly giving him the impression that she might cut his throat while he slept. *In fact*, he thought eyeing her surreptitiously, *she might well wait as long as it took for my guard to go down. Years if need be, and then stick a dagger under my ear.*

"Humour me and answer a question," Alienor said.

"Very well." Gregory tried to ignore the way de Gilbert was violently shaking his head.

"Well, then, Sir Maudesley. Are you wanting to marry me or is it my dowry you're marrying?" Alienor said.

A small voice at the back of Gregory's head, which sounded disturbingly like Fletcher, begged him to say something flattering and meaningless. But Gregory found he couldn't do it. Well aware that he was ruining his chance to marry his way out of disaster, he answered truthfully.

"The dowry is the greater attraction, Lady." He thought about adding a few words to say that any man would be glad to have such an intelligent, beautiful, witty... No, he could not do it. "But you would be accorded every respect and honour due to you as my wife, regardless of how or why, or...or anything which came before."

Baron de Gilbert threw his hands up as if to say he was done with the whole business.

Alienor cast a measuring glance over Gregory, leaving him in no doubt that she was not especially pleased by what she saw. "He'll do. Arrange the wedding as you see fit, Uncle."

Gregory couldn't make sense of her words for a moment. He'd been thinking about how to exit with some dignity intact. But she had agreed to marry him. He could raise the inheritance fee. "Lady?"

Alienor gave him a look that said all too plainly that she hoped he wasn't this stupid all the time. "We'll be wed. That is what you want, is it not?"

"Er...yes... That is..."

"Very well then. I'll see you at the wedding, Sir Maudesley." She exited the room as briskly as she'd entered it, leaving her confused suitor and stunned guardian behind her.

7.

28th May, 1381

The small entourage reached the outskirts of London late the following day. Drum plodded on valiantly but the big horse was made for the heat of battle, not hours of steady riding. Even with Gregory stopping to walk and water him often, the courser was obviously tired. Gregory reflected that he was no longer a youth himself – he'd felt every inch of the last few miles and almost wished there was a second ambler so he might have enjoyed a smoother ride. Young Cuthbert, on the other hand, seemed unnaturally alert and full of enthusiastic curiosity for someone who had spent all day in the saddle. Gregory glowered at him. As he'd suspected, the ambler he'd reclaimed from the thieves hadn't noticed the extra weight of the boy. Cuthbert was all eyes and elbows and knees.

"Now what are you grinning about?" Gregory said gruffly.

"It's an adventure, my lord. I never been to London afore. I never left Littlefolds," Cuthbert enthused.

"It's just another dirty city, not something to get your braies in a knot over," Gregory grumbled. "Stop bloody smiling. It makes you look like a simpleton."

"Yes, my lord," Cuthbert said brightly. The grin stayed in place. Young fool probably wasn't even aware of it.

Gregory decided that he would sell Cuthbert's indenture to the first person who made him a decent offer. The lad was clearly unhinged. No one should be that cheerful all the time. He was beginning to see why the smith had beaten the boy. Cuthbert was completely impervious to Gregory's ill temper and sharp words. As if the boy thought him a good master, rather than a fearsome, grizzled warrior. The knight wasn't sure he could tolerate much more of that.

Gregory had seen a great many cities, both in England and

overseas, and while England might have nothing to show more fair than its capital, he was not especially moved. It was an ugly pile when all was said and done. Long ago, London had been much smaller and encircled with Roman walls. Now it sprawled across the Thames in both directions, breaching those walls and swallowing neighbouring towns like a sow devouring her offspring. Westminster had been ingested in just such a way and now formed the heart of both London itself and government in England. Some way off, Gregory saw smoke rising from what must be the brickfields. In another direction lay the heaving district of Southwark.

Cuthbert goggled at the city, then swivelled in his saddle to stare perplexed at the unbroken green meadows and copses that stretched for mile on mile behind them. Two such different realities could hardly be expected to share the same world, his expression said. Gregory realised again how reckless it had been to burden himself with the boy. Cuthbert had spent all his life in one small town. Surely Gregory would only need to turn his back on the lad for a moment and Cuthbert would be fleeced right out of his shirt and skin.

"Heed me now," Gregory said sternly. "You're not to go wandering off by yourself."

"No, my lord," Cuthbert said, eyes wide.

"You're to let no one take the reins of our mounts, save you or me, you hear?"

"Would someone try to steal 'em?"

"Most likely Drum wouldn't go and would take a chunk out of whoever tried, but I'd rather it didn't come to that. If you lose that nag, you'll be walking back to Essex."

"Yes, my lord."

"And no matter what story some poor, young woman spins for you, you're not to follow her down any alleys. I don't care if she has six sick mothers or eighteen dying babies, you stay put, understand? I don't care what she promises you or how pretty she is."

"Y-yes, my lord," Cuthbert frowned a little as if the thought were both fascinating and mildly terrifying. "Them that goes with these girls, what happens to them?"

"Sometimes they get 'skinned' of their clothes and valuables – not that you have any. Sometimes they just get a knife in the ribs." Gregory gave Cuthbert a very stern look. "But youngsters like you get sold to brothels. There's a certain type of man that would pay well for a boy your age, no questions asked."

Cuthbert's eyes widened even further and his lips formed a quivering line.

"Not that you're much to look at," Gregory went on ruthlessly, determined to make the boy careful if he couldn't make him well behaved. "But that won't matter much to the sort of clientele that frequents those places."

Cuthbert went very white under his collection of bruises. For the first time there was no cheeky smile lurking at the corners of the boy's mouth. Gregory shifted in his saddle, uncomfortable without knowing why. The boy did need to be warned after all.

"You don't need to worry about me, my lord," Cuthbert said, in a small, clear voice.

"I'm not worried about you," Gregory barked, immediately incensed. "I'm only worried about losing the shilling I paid for you, before you work off its value."

"Yes, my lord," Cuthbert said. The ill-concealed smile was back.

Gregory glowered at him and urged Drum to a trot. "Keep up, boy."

They were forced to slow as they reached London Bridge. The foot traffic grew thick and Gregory ordered Cuthbert to stay close. The only thing denser than the throngs of city dwellers was the smell. Gutter ordure – both animal and human, not so fresh fish, meat hanging from sellers hooks and gleaming with the rainbow sheen of early spoilage, the reek of tanneries and the savoury scent of pies, all clashed against the low tide smell from the Thames and the hot stench of many people all living and working in the same few square miles.

"How can they do it?" Cuthbert said, in horrified wonder. "How do folks live on top of each other like this?"

Gregory was tired and irritable, not at all in a mood to humour the irrepressible wretch. He turned to snarl a terse command for

Cuthbert to shut up but found the boy's attention had been drawn to the mouth of an alley. A girl only a few years older than Cuthbert stood there. Her gown was loosened at the neck and had half fallen from one pale shoulder. She had a pretty, somewhat grimy face and fair hair. She smiled at Cuthbert, beckoning to him. Cuthbert gulped audibly and set his blazing face forward, so that he looked straight between his mare's twitching ears.

Perhaps the lad listened more than he was given credit for, Gregory mused. And it was only natural he should be curious about the city. He turned his attention back to the direction they were heading in.

It took them several hours to cross the city, by which time it was far too late to go to Westminster and beg an audience. Gregory could hardly present himself in his filthy, travel worn state in any case. It rankled but he would have to part with more precious coin and take a room in an inn so that he could wash, rest and make himself presentable for the morrow.

Despite the crowds, there were whole streets of houses that had been left empty and unlived in for at least three decades. These patches of desolation cropped up all over the city and had a melancholy, resentful air. Doors and windows were roughly boarded shut like bandaged eyes.

"What happened?" Cuthbert shuddered.

Gregory glanced at him. "You've heard of the Black Pestilence, boy?"

Cuthbert nodded.

Gregory indicated the empty houses that rose on either side of them. "That's what happens when for every three people in a city, plague kills two of them."

"Are they...are they haunted?" Cuthbert said in a hushed voice.

"Don't talk such nonsense," Gregory said harshly, but the empty houses made him uneasy too and he was glad when they reached West Cheap, leaving the deserted buildings behind them.

***

The Half Moon inn stood on the corner of Petticoat Lane, a notorious brothel district. Gregory supposed it wasn't a respectable establishment but it was cheap, even with stabling for Drum and the ambler mare – which Cuthbert had named 'Patience', with typical though misplaced optimism. Cowed by the noise and raucous laughter of the tap room, Cuthbert elected to sleep in the stables with the horses. Gregory's head ached and he was glad to see the back of the lad and his inane chatter for the night. He'd bought meat pies at the West Cheap market. The pies had been slightly stale but still good, and he'd eaten his with only slightly less relish than Cuthbert had wolfed his own.

Few travellers could afford a private chamber at even the meanest tavern. Most were forced to share with other travellers, paying additional fees for use of an actual bed, or less to bed down on the floor. It wasn't unusual for several families to find themselves sharing, or for pilgrims and travellers to only hire half a bed and share it with a complete stranger. Women and men tended to be segregated unless they were a married couple, though fewer women travelled any distance. Those who did were usually wealthy and high born, and consequently not to be found frequenting inns in the brothel district.

Gregory had not hesitated to use his pull as nobility to secure a private chamber at a price he could afford. The beleaguered and resentful innkeeper had shown him to a narrow, dim room that was scarcely more than a closet. The bed was barely long enough for Gregory to lie fully stretched out upon it and the straw mattress, under the worn sheet, was old and lumpy. But it seemed clean enough and there was a bolt on the inside of the chamber door. Nor, as a noble, was he required to share, something Gregory was especially leery of now that he was so close to completing his objective. Since the robbery, the money had taken on a quasi-life of its own at the back of his mind. As if it would find ways to become lost or re-stolen or even to waste itself, until he could no longer pay the inheritance fee. He had never expected to be so keen to rid himself of three hundred pounds. Certainly not to see his money swallowed by the royal treasury.

Gregory stripped down to his shirt and braies. He set his sword on the floor beside the bed and slipped his dagger under the pillow – old habits died hard. Then he cast himself onto his back on the mattress and closed his eyes. From the common room below came the rhythmic thumping that accompanied the singing of some bawdy song. From further down the hall came the unmistakeable sounds of someone enjoying one of the inn's rooms rented by the hour – and the girl who came with the room to 'see to any special needs'. Gregory snorted. It was a neat piece of sophistry. Hover on the borders of respectability as a business by not being a brothel and yet share a brothel's clientele by renting the room rather than the girl. He tuned all the noise out and for the first time, allowed himself to think about what he would do when his inheritance was finally his.

There were flocks to replenish and fields that must be tilled. It was late in the year to begin much of it but with back breaking effort and enough good workers, they might manage to grow enough food to keep themselves and still pay taxes next year. Of course, he no longer had many workers at all, let alone good ones so that was the first problem. Parts of the castle needed shoring up until repairs could be carried out too. He wondered if his wife's dowry would stretch just a little further. Damn William for running the estate into the ground! And damn his father for allowing his favourite son to do it!

Gregory was under no illusions about the tedious struggle that lay ahead. There would be no more sudden influxes of cash. He could hardly marry another wealthy bride. Which brought him to the question of Alienor. Here, Gregory drew a blank. He did not have the faintest idea what to do about his shrewish wife. His last thought as sleep claimed him was that he would rather have her as an ally than an enemy.

8.

1st May, 1381
Three weeks earlier

The wedding took place on Mayday. Alienor looked disquietingly lovely in her dark blue gown. Instead of a veil, she wore her hair loose, with hawthorn blossoms woven into the tiny plaits that caught the dark mass back from her face. Gregory couldn't help but notice that his bride also wore a very cool, cynical expression that matched his own feelings too well for him to delude himself that Alienor took any pleasure in the occasion.

A peasant wedding was a simple affair. The couple agreed they wished to be married and then declared that they recognised each other as husband and wife. It was rare for a priest to bless a union – marriage, after all, was not the province of the Church, though no doubt the Church would very much like to add weddings to its list of ways to generate income. If there was any sort of celebration, it was a mild affair. Often there was nothing to mark the occasion at all.

However, nobility were expected to wed with more fanfare, the pageantry commensurate with their station and wealth. It was traditional for the bridegroom to furnish a wedding breakfast not merely for his family and that of his intended, but for his entire household and as many of his tenants as could attend. Gregory had resented this fact intensely, even as he had scraped up enough resources for a modest banquet. It would not do to insult his new kinsmen, or his wife. In the end, however, it was a mean and cheerless affair. Gregory was not yet known, let alone liked or respected by his remaining tenants and bondsmen. Alienor's guests consisted of her uncle, aunt, two of her cousins and a lady's maid of the chamber, who had travelled from the Marches with her, and spoke with an accent that was

49

utterly impenetrable to Gregory. No one was inclined to dance, which was just as well since there were no musicians.

Alienor was quiet but her grey eyes flashed. She was clearly furious, although she had gone through the simple wedding ceremony in the castle doorway with perfect composure and willing resignation, if not enthusiasm. Gregory, hardly in a better humour than his new bride, nevertheless made a few attempts to engage her in conversation.

"It was a fair day for a wedding at least," was his first bumbling attempt.

Alienor arched an eyebrow at him. "Please do not trouble yourself with commonplaces on my account, husband. I am quite content with silence." The slight stress on the word 'husband' left Gregory in no doubt that she found idea of being married in general, or to him in particular, utterly distasteful. "Besides," she went on, "you know what they say about marriages begun at such a season."

Gregory frowned. Until that moment, it hadn't occurred to him that it was a holiday. No one was celebrating it. "What do they say?"

A sly smile curved Alienor's lips. "Marry in May, regret it for aye."

"Superstition," Gregory snapped. "And if it *were* true, would that please you, my lady?"

Alienor sipped her wine demurely. "Depends on how it ends, I suppose."

"Is that why you've got May blossom in your hair? Bringing ill intent into the marriage before it even starts?" He glowered at her.

Alienor gave a hard, contemptuous little laugh. "This is how it is done in the Marchs. The bride wears flowers. If I'd known it would fright you, I'd have had Mairi dress my hair differently."

Gregory fought to hide his irritation. Why did she have to be so provoking? He hadn't dragged her into this. She'd agreed to the union of her own free will. And he'd not deceived her as to his motives, though by God, if he could have had her dowry without taking her as part of the bargain, he would have done so. For all her loveliness, Alienor had a sharp tongue and the disconcerting habit of speaking her mind. Add that to the fact that he suspected his wife might be cleverer he was, and she was an unappealing prospect indeed.

"I hope you will be comfortable here, my lady," Gregory forced himself to grind out. He took hold of his goblet and rose, leaving his half eaten meal on the platter. He'd married her. He'd hold to his vow and see her sheltered. But God's Wounds he didn't have to sit there and endure her working off her ill temper with sly, sharp words to him.

There was, of course, the matter of the dowry. Gregory had expected to receive it from de Gilbert shortly after the vows were made, but the baron had only given him one third of the promised amount. Uncouth and unpolished as he was, Gregory had held back from humiliating his wife less than an hour into their marriage by openly demanding why the sum was short. Now seemed as good a time as any to speak to the baron and find out when the remainder would be forthcoming. Later, there would be the wedding night to get through. He found he wasn't looking forward to that with much anticipation at all.

***

Gregory approached the lord's bed chamber with something that felt suspiciously like trepidation. At least the diminished staff, lack of family and generally mean banquet meant that there was no carousing. No merry crowd of well-wishers and pranksters surrounding himself or the bride. No one to see the bride put to bed or ensure that he joined her. However, an attempt to sleep elsewhere would certainly be noticed and gossiped about. Gregory was already conscious of the chatter surrounding his new wife and well aware that none of it was favourable. Alienor's apparent indifference to it rankled. Did she care nothing for his honour and reputation, even if she would cast her own to the winds?

And then there was the matter of whether or not the girl was already with child. Gregory suspected she was. If Alienor had not been so frank about why her guardian was so keen for her to marry, then there might have been reasonable doubt as to the bastard's true parentage. Gregory could have lived with the speculation and would have raised the child as his, although he would have prayed for a girl so he did not have to explain why a first born son could not inherit. But everyone knew and would be counting moons to see how fast a child arrived.

He paused outside the chamber door, mastering his ill temper. She had not deceived him. Not tried to foist a bastard on him without his knowledge, by bringing a cuckoo into his nest. It did not especially trouble him that she'd had a previous lover. The priests might say what they liked about it being better to marry than to burn, but in Gregory's experience most people asked forgiveness rather than sought permission. Nobles guarded their daughters carefully, but among the lower classes it was hardly a scandal. So he could be reasonable – if only there had been no gossip.

The chamber door opened, revealing Alienor in a sheer, white shift and an irritable expression.

"Have you lost your way, my lord? You need only take another two steps. Four at most." She left the door open and walked back to stand before the huge feather bed – one of the few things of value that William had not sold or gambled away.

Gregory noticed idly that someone had scattered more flower petals on the coverlet and that there were branches of May flowers and apple blossom over the tester. He glowered, thinking there was little need for charms of fertility when the bride was already expecting.

Alienor lifted an eyebrow in that infuriatingly superior manner he was becoming so familiar with. "And still you stand there. Perhaps you mean to sleep across the threshold like a faithful hound?"

Gregory's temper flared and he slammed the door behind him. Alienor paled a little but her eyes glinted wickedly and the corners of her mouth twitched in a slight smile.

Gregory glared at her. "I'd advise you not to make needling me one of your delights. You'll not like the outcome."

Her smile grew cold and scornful. "A threat, my lord?"

"An observation. I've no need to make threats."

She eyed him from top to bottom, her expression unreadable. He wondered what fresh flaws she was finding in him, but all she said was, "perhaps not."

He noticed her hands had clenched into fists at her sides. Either she meant to hit him or she was trying to stop them shaking. The shift she wore didn't do much to hide her figure. She was very slender. If she was with child, it was early days yet. Perhaps she wasn't? Or perhaps she had been but had lost it? If only there was some way to know for sure.

"I presume you know what you're doing," Alienor interrupted his musings in a business like tone.

"What?" Gregory said, startled.

Alienor gave him a very sardonic look. "I'll not believe you if you try to tell me you've never lain with a woman before, my lord." She sat on the edge of the bed. "The hour grows late. Perhaps we could get on with it."

Gregory might have bristled at her tone, which was one of command rather than enquiry, except that he saw how white her face had grown. Her lips were pressed together in a thin line that stole their natural redness. He'd been half ready to throttle her a moment ago – his new wife with her air of condescending to his level. He'd also been half ready to fall on her ravenously, because for all he disliked the girl, she was lovely and she was now his wife. Apparently she was also willing, despite her disdain. Except he'd just had a glimpse beneath her bold words.

"Not tonight." Gregory thought he caught a flash of something like relief in her eyes, quickly buried beneath more scorn. She was probably thinking of her lover. He felt a sudden absurd stab of jealousy that she should prefer a man who abandoned her and her unborn bastard over her lawful husband, and tramped to the far side of the bed, shedding outer clothing with no care for the delicate cloth or its embroidery.

"My lord?" Alienor said, sounding gratifyingly confused.

"Put out the light and go to sleep," Gregory returned tersely. He got into bed and turned on his side away from her. The bed was so broad there could have been three newly married couples in it and they still wouldn't touch each other. He was confident Alienor would keep to her own side.

"Very well." The room plunged into darkness lit only by the reddish glow of embers in the hearth.

She moved so softly that he did not hear her cross the room to the bed, but he was intensely aware of her presence. It seemed she paused by the bed, hesitating. He thought about jibing her with her own words about sleeping places and loyal hounds but held his tongue. She was so light she barely disturbed the mattress or the coverlet as she got in on the far side of the bed.

They did not speak and Gregory's prediction was correct; Alienor stayed well away from him. Gregory reflected that there was one sure way for him to know if any child she bore was his, and that was the reason he would not demand his marital rights of her. It seemed a sound plan in the quiet of his own mind. He chose not to examine too closely his other motives. That he preferred the women he lay with to be not merely resigned but eager. That he would not stoop to compete for his wife's affections with a feckless and absent rival. Besides, he would soon have the entire dowry. He could seek an audience with the king and pay his inheritance relief. Maudesley estate would be truly his. It would be prosperous once more. Time enough to worry about the getting of heirs when there was something worth them inheriting.

9.

12ᵗʰ June, 1381

Gregory rose from the bench and began to pace. He knew the seneschal hated it when he did that and irritating the seneschal was all that was currently keeping Gregory sane. It had seemed a simple enough task; seek an audience with the king, make an oath of fealty, pay his inheritance relief – finally that wretched silver would be out of his possession – and have the king confirm him as heir to the Maudesley estate. He'd even expected to wait. A day, perhaps two. Instead, Gregory had lost the last of May and the first week and a half of June. He found himself fantasising about wringing the seneschal's scrawny neck with increasing frequency. It would wipe the look of disapproval off the man's face at least.

A page entered the antechamber on hasty pattering feet. Those seated around the room, hoping to petition the king, looked up sharply like hounds that have heard a command. Gregory paused in his pacing. The page cast a nervous glance at the company – a couple of merchants, a guild master, a wealthy widow, an abbot and Gregory – then hastily murmured his message in the seneschal's ear. The seneschal straightened as the page beat a hasty retreat. The same scrawny throat Gregory had been thinking about crushing, bobbed convulsively as the seneschal swallowed. The news was not going to be good.

"His majesty regrets that he is unable to see you today..." the seneschal began.

Gregory swore, causing the widow to stare at him in alarm and edge away.

"He has been forced to repair to the Tower until further notice..." Another hard swallow. "The rebels have almost reached the city."

Gregory strode out of the Royal Palace, not bothering to hear more. His fury cast an invisible nimbus around him as he stormed to the stables. No one who saw the big man, moving like an angry bear and fulminating strange incantations under his breath, in which various saints and their body parts played the principal roles, dared to approach him. He frightened the stable lads into fetching his horse and headed towards *The Half Moon*.

It had all started with John Brampton. Gregory had been waiting for an audience with the king on the second day of June when there had been an outcry and a scuffle with the guards in the corridor. Brampton and his co-horts had arrived, demanding to be taken before the council at once. Gregory, who had not felt at all inclined to obey the seneschal's entreaties to come away from the door, had observed that Brampton looked battered and ill-used. A middle aged man, running slightly to fat, but well dressed and otherwise possessed of all his parts. Except that his face was severely bruised and he held himself like one who has suffered an injury to the ribs. Gregory recognised that particular stoop.

"They're in open rebellion!" Brampton cried, heedless of how his voice carried. "They mean to march, I'm certain of it. We must warn the king...the council..."

It was then that Gregory realised where he'd heard the name Brampton before. The village of Littlefolds had been full of hostile whispers the tax collector from London and favourable mutterings about the cleric, John Ball.

"They must be stopped!" Brampton shouted at the guard, who was trying to placate him. "They killed my clerks!"

Gregory's eyebrows rose. Brampton was well-connected both at court and with parliament. If rebel townsfolk had attacked him and killed his staff while he was trying to collect unpaid taxes, then the situation was serious. Gregory had seen examples of the undercurrents of discontent in every town and village he passed on the way to London. It was partly why he'd had to wait so long to see the king.

The council had been in session with the fourteen-year-old monarch and – rumour had it – with his mother, Joan, Countess of Kent and Princess of Wales, ever since Brampton's return.

Gregory had doubted the rebels would get far. No doubt the band would tear itself apart before it ever reached London. Or so he'd thought until a few days ago, when reports of organised and armed rebel bands had trickled in. The Kentish rebels in particular had been whipped into a fury by a man named Wat Tyler. Reports were confused and contradictory, but Tyler had emerged as a figurehead of the rebellion. The rebels were heading towards London and Tyler, along with other leaders, would make sure they did not disband before they achieved their aim. Whatever that was.

It occurred to Gregory, now, that spending more time on the streets than necessary was foolish and he urged Drum to a trot. Any rebellion would be crushed of course, but before that there would be fighting, destruction of property, fire. There was something about a revolt that brought out the moonwits and the truly nasty specimens of humanity who usually hid from common sight. A breakdown in law and order meant that London had just become much less safe, and it had not been a place to lower your guard before that.

Gregory had been in sieges on both sides of the walls; he had acted as a bodyguard to a highly unpopular count; he'd seen most of the varied shades of red that war came in. But the one time he had genuinely been afraid he might die, was during a bread riot in Carcassone. There had been a grain shortage due to blighted crops. The price of bread doubled, then tripled overnight. Even the rough bread peasants ate was too expensive for any but the very wealthy to buy, and a hasty new law prevented them buying grain to make their own. It had taken less than a day before the hungry populace was a seething, mindless mob bent on violence and destruction. Gregory had led a militia to protect the main keep while relief arrived. He never wanted to have a fight with hungry people who had nothing to lose again. He reached West Cheap and dismounted at the stables. Drum snorted, butting his nose against Gregory's chest.

"Cuthbert? Where are you lad?"

There was a scuffling noise from the hay loft overhead and the boy slid down the ladder to land untidily at Gregory's feet.

"Did you see the king yet? Is he really not much older than me?" Cuthbert said enthusiastically.

"No," Gregory snapped. "There's been news, though."

"'Bout them rebels?" Cuthbert said.

"What have you heard?"

"Angry people coming here from Kent. Something about taxes."

Gregory nodded. "It's not just Kent. Essex too." It occurred to him there could be people from his own lands who'd thrown their lot in with the rebels. "I want you to stay off the streets."

"Yes, my lord," Cuthbert said, frowning.

"They'll probably head to Westminster or Guildhall. But if they look to be heading this way, you're to take Drum and that ridiculous nag and get out of the City."

"But why?" Cuthbert did not look happy at the prospect of abandoning his master.

"I've seen something like this before," Gregory said. "If it gets bad enough, they won't stop for anyone. They'll use fire. You're sitting in a tinderbox, lad."

Cuthbert gulped.

"Do as you're told," Gregory said, cuffing him lightly on the shoulder. "Disobey my orders and you'll wish you hadn't."

"Yes, my lord." Cuthbert took hold of Drum's reins.

Gregory slapped Drum's neck and strode off in search of the bar. He did not intend to get drunk but an ale was certainly called for. Perhaps two. Then he could forget the frustrating business of his inheritance, banish Alienor from his thoughts and convince himself that his concern had been for his very expensive warhorse rather than his very cheap bondsman.

***

Gregory was well into his third ale with the sharp edges of reality blurring pleasantly, when the girl approached him. She stood over him, one hand resting on a slim hip, lips curling up in an insinuating smile. Gregory recognised her as the girl he'd chased out of his room twice now. He supposed that he'd been a disappointment in terms of earning extra coin. He doubted many patrons who rented a room turned down the girl inside.

The girl lifted the ale jug she carried. "Something to wet your throat, my lord?" Her tone promised all kinds of wicked diversions.

For a moment Gregory was half tempted. It would hardly be the first time and there was a kind of honesty in exchanging money for what was merely another service. It had been a while and lacking a violent outlet, Gregory could certainly use another method for bleeding off his frustration. The girl's smile widened as he hesitated. She had dark hair, like Alienor's, though not as thick and glossy. The thought acted like a dash of cold water. Gregory set his ale mug down and pushed the half-finished drink away.

"I've nothing for you, girl."

The girl looked him up and down ostentatiously. "I wouldn't say that, my lord."

Gregory was struck once again with the similarity to his wife. Alienor had given him a once over in the same manner, although her appraisal had been decidedly unimpressed. This girl's look was appreciative. Well of course it was – she was paid to keep grizzled old sods like him happy.

"Get along with you," Gregory said, not unkindly.

The young prostitute dropped her arch manner, regarding him ruefully. "You're a tough nut to crack, my lord. Is all well with you?"

Gregory smiled grimly. "I imagine you're not refused often, but have no fear. I doubt your next mark will be able to resist your charms."

The girl tossed her head pertly. "A pretty speech, my lord. I'll try to recover from the disappointment." She winked at him and bore the jug away to try her luck with a less unyielding target.

Gregory glanced at the ale mug again, tempted to just finish it. The coin was already spent after all. But no. It would lead to a fourth and a fifth. Bad enough that waiting on the king's pleasure – or his council's at least – meant that he'd been haemorrhaging a steady flow of cash for the last two weeks. No need to add to that with debauchery or drunkenness. And that was the only reason he'd refused the advances of the dark haired prostitute. Gregory glowered sightlessly at the half full ale mug, thinking curses at his wife, who had inexplicably trotted into his thoughts again. A disturbance on the other side of the room drew his attention.

Cuthbert made an ill-timed dive between two inebriated tradesmen at the bar, knocking into one and causing him to slop ale down the front of his tunic. Gregory watched as Cuthbert dodged a vengeful kick and burrowed a trail of disturbance through the room, coming to a halt in front of him.

"My lord! Quick!"

"Cuthbert, what are you doing here?" Gregory made no attempt to move. He had no intention of going anywhere, quickly or otherwise.

"There's a man in the alley! Robbers have set on him! He might die!"

"Why should that concern me?" Gregory said.

"But...you're a *knight*." Cuthbert's eyes were wide, full of earnest belief in what was good and right. "Aren't you going to help him?"

"It's his own bloody fault if he was walking the streets in the current climate. I'm not surprised he came to misadventure," Gregory said dismissively. "Go back to the stables."

"But...but my lord..." Cuthbert's angular, unlovely face filled with disappointment.

No, Gregory thought, it was worse than that. It was as if he'd managed to crush the boy in a way that the beatings of the blacksmith never had. As if the bot had lost some sense of the essential rightness of the world.

Gregory suddenly remembered being a lad of the same age. How ardently he'd believed such things about his older brother. How he had believed them for himself. Reading had not come easily to him as it had to William. Nor had swordplay. He'd slaved at the latter until William, four years his senior and reckoned to be the best of his age amongst the squires, had deigned to cross blades with him. William had won bout after bout, until Gregory, who was almost of a height with his brother despite being only fourteen, had managed with herculean effort

60

to disarm him. He still remembered the freezing smile William had given him. How he'd been ready to hear praise from his hero. And how William had caught hold of his sword arm, and casually broken it. Gregory had spent the rest of that summer learning to use a sword in his left hand – which had turned out to be an advantage since he was now almost as good with either hand. But his fourteen-year-old self had lost his unquestioning faith in the Code that day. It would take almost another seven years before his admiration for William died too.

Selling his sword had stripped away any last illusions. Humans were uniquely suited to their own interests and to inventing new and terrible ways to harm each other. Didn't matter if you were noble or common. Or royal, for that matter. So the fragile, nebulous imaginings of what knighthood and chivalric code meant had fallen apart like cobweb. It was just as well. Idealists didn't survive. The Code was a lie.

And yet there it was, bright but slowly dying in that scrawny servant boy's eyes.

Cuthbert turned and started making his way dejectedly back across the tavern. Gregory looked into his ale, then slammed the damn thing down so hard the mug cracked. He went after Cuthbert and people got out of his way as they would not for the boy. He clapped a hand heavily down on the boy's bird-boned shoulder, glowering at him in a way that forbade any comment.

"Show me where, then."

Cuthbert's face lit up and he led Gregory at a run down two nearby alleys.

"I told you to stay off the streets," Gregory began angrily.

The sounds of a scuffle interrupted him. Cuthbert pointed around a corner and Gregory peered into the mouth of an even darker, narrower alley. It stank of piss. The ground was unpaved, a dark soup of mud and ordure. A sparely built man of medium height struggled against three assailants, who struck him casually as they rummaged about his person for valuables.

"Stay here," Gregory said, not even glancing at Cuthbert to see if his order was obeyed. He was unaware that he was smiling as he piled into the nearest attacker. The luckless thief found himself spun away from his target, and thrust face first into the wall of the nearest building. Gregory laced the fingers of one hand through the attacker's greasy hair, cupping the back of his skull almost tenderly as he pulled him back again. The man managed one panicked, wheezy gasp before Gregory smashed his face into the wall with even more force and he crumpled senseless in the filth of the alley.

There was a whoop of triumph from the mouth of the alleyway – apparently staying put was as far as Cuthbert was willing to go. Gregory ignored it, turning to his next opponent. He had his sword and his dagger with him, in a pinch he had a long, thin bladed knife concealed in his boot. But Gregory didn't want to use his blades if he could avoid it. He didn't necessarily want to kill them. Just break a few bones or loosen a few teeth.

"Who in God's name are you?" The next attacker said, less alarmed and more affronted at Gregory's interference. He was a tall, rail thin man with a drooping moustache.

"Don't bring the Almighty into it. He has nothing to do with what's about to happen here," Gregory said ominously.

"Bugger that!" Moustache said and sliced an arc towards Gregory's face with a short curved knife.

Gregory pulled his head back out of range then closed the distance, catching the back of Moustache's wrist with one hand to hold the arm rigid at the widest point of the arc, then slamming the heel of his other hand through Moustache's locked elbow. There was a sickening wet snap and Moustache screamed, dropping the knife. Gregory kicked it behind him, grabbing Moustache's shoulders and ramming a knee up into his groin. Moustache had already been folding up in agony but with such encouragement applied to his genitals, he dropped like a stone.

Gregory was aware of a soaring sense of well-being. God was in his heaven and the world made sense. There was no wrangling with customs or courtesies. No worry about grain yield or bushels of hay. Just the pure, simple red joy of violence richly deserved and honestly meted.

A movement in his peripheral vision made him jerk sideways

and the stinging kiss of a blade caught the edge of his ear rather than his throat or face. The third assailant didn't have many teeth. Gregory could see that clearly because he was standing there with his mouth open, horrified that Gregory had avoided what should have been a fatal blow. Toothless brandished the knife but his hand shook. Gregory batted the blade contemptuously to one side and followed it with a blow to the man's jaw, which Toothless dodged clumsily. He possessed slightly more wit than his cohorts and took to his heels.

Gregory sighed. Why did one always run? You'd almost believe they didn't want to beaten into a bloody pulp. Gregory had no intention of running after the thief. Wasn't as if any of his own property had been stolen.

"My...script..."

Up until that point, Gregory hadn't considered the thieves' victim at all. He'd all but forgotten how he came to be in the middle of a brawl, in his enjoyment of finally bleeding off frustration in violence. Now, he looked down at the older man, intending say that he had no intention of chasing the miscreant, only to realise that he recognised him. It was the poet who'd found him in the horse trough

"You!" Gregory got no further. There was a yelp and a crash from the end of the alley. He'd forgotten that the running thief was heading straight towards his servant. Gregory whirled, ready to chase the thief after all, only to see Cuthbert standing over the prone body of the runner. Torchlight gleamed off the sharp, curved edge of the knife Gregory had kicked aside earlier.

"I got him, my lord!" Cuthbert called, voice high with excitement.

Gregory looked heavenward for patience, muttering under his breath about scrawny boys who were too stupid to just stay out of the way. He hauled the poet to his feet.

"Are you hurt?" he said gruffly.

"Bruises and bumps," the poet said. "My script though..."

"Cuthbert, did that dog turd have a bag on him?" Gregory called.

"It's here, my lord." Cuthbert sounded as if he thought a late night scuffle in a filthy alley was the high point of his life so far.

"Oh thank the Almighty," the poet said fervently.

"I would," Gregory replied drily, "but everything happened so fast, I must have missed his presence during the excitement."

The poet looked at Gregory sternly for a moment, then threw back his head and laughed. Cuthbert gingerly toed the thief who'd tried to run. The man groaned incoherently, so the lad hadn't killed him.

Gregory cuffed Cuthbert lightly around the back of the head. "What did I tell you about staying out of it?"

"You said to stay here, my lord. And I did," Cuthbert said, utterly unfazed by the knight's disapproval. "And you kicked the knife towards me. Did you not mean for me to have it, my lord?"

The poet began to chuckle again, glancing at Gregory in a sly, astute way the knight didn't care for at all.

"What did you do to him?" Gregory nodded to the fallen thief.

"Oh! I didn't stab him, my lord. I tripped him up and he hit his head on that step," Cuthbert said. "Can I keep the knife?"

"Saints preserve us," Gregory muttered.

He could see the poet more clearly once they were out under the torchlight. The poet's face was bruised and dirty, and a cut oozed sluggishly over one eyebrow. He looked shaken but seemed to be regaining his equanimity with remarkable speed. Perhaps he'd had some military experience in his youth, Gregory mused. The smaller man should not have been able to hold off three armed attackers for that long otherwise. Not with mere scrapes to show for it.

"What brought you out on such an evening as this? Have you not heard what's happening outside the city?" Gregory said.

The poet shrugged. "It was just such business that brought me from home. There were messages awaiting my collection."

"And you had no servant to send for them?" Gregory said.

The poet gave him a dry smile. "None such as I would trust with such delicate work."

"Do you live nearby?" He cast a doubtful look at the poet's clothes which were plain but of very fine material. It was unlikely he was a regular in West Cheap.

"My home is in Aldgate," the poet said. He had taken his script back from Cuthbert and was checking the contents with a frown.

"Is it all there?" Cuthbert said.

"What? Oh, yes. Thank you, lad. That was some neat footwork."

Cuthbert beamed.

"Don't encourage him," Gregory said. "Aldgate is a tidy distance from here. You'll need to get that head wound seen to before you travel so far."

"He should come back to the inn with us, my lord," Cuthbert piped up.

Gregory had been thinking along the same lines but it didn't stop him feeling irritated at Cuthbert suggesting it. The last thing he needed was more strays or people in need. All Gregory wanted was his inheritance, was that so much to ask? And yet at every step of the way, more disaster. Perhaps God *had* turned His face from the Maudesley line. Gregory turned in the direction of *the Half Moon*, Cuthbert trotting happily at his heels.

"I'll admit some wine would be welcome just now," the poet said, matching his stride. "Since we are to drink together, may I have the name of the…noble knight to whom I am so indebted?"

Gregory opened his mouth to say something gruff but Cuthbert was already speaking.

"My master is Sir Gregory, Baronet Maudesley of Wynnstree, noble sir," Cuthbert said proudly.

Gregory suppressed a groan. He really would have to beat some manners into the infuriating boy. The poet looked amused but accepted the introduction in the spirit Cuthbert intended it. Gregory wished they'd both just bugger off.

"Then I am pleased to make your acquaintance, Baronet Maudesley," the poet said. "My name is Chaucer. My friends call me Geoffrey."

"Not you, boy. You'll address him as Master Chaucer," Gregory said to Cuthbert, who had lit up at the idea of being counted amongst the poet's friends. "I'm not a baronet yet."

"I see," Chaucer said.

They had reached the inn and the rowdy cheering from inside was almost as welcome as the wide beam of orange light that sliced through the darkness from the open door. Gregory waited to see if Master Chaucer, who was clearly wealthy and well connected, would demure at setting foot in a tavern that was only a notch above being a bawdy house. The poet didn't hesitate, however, and Gregory wondered if Chaucer was often called upon to frequent dens of low repute in the course of 'collecting messages'. Thinking on it, *the Crossed Keys*, where he'd first met Chaucer, had been on the shadier side of respectable.

Gregory caught Cuthbert by the collar of his tunic and propelled him over to the table in the corner. It had been Gregory's preferred seat these past two weeks and the other patrons had learned that the knight did not take kindly to company, nor to having his table appropriated. A group of local tradesmen had thought Gregory retired for the night and settled themselves down, but one look at the big knight's expression had them all hurrying to collect mugs and make a tactical withdrawal.

"There," Gregory indicated that Master Chaucer should be seated before thrusting Cuthbert onto a stool. "Sit still." He caught the attention of a passing serving girl and ordered food and drink. Bowls of what passed for stew and hunks of bread arrived, along with well-watered ale.

"You'll have to make do," Gregory said to Chaucer. "I don't dislike you enough yet to suggest you try the sort of wine they serve in this establishment."

"Given the circumstances of our first meeting, that's most generous of you, Sir Maudesley," Chaucer said wryly.

"Do you already know Master Chaucer, my lord?" Cuthbert said, forgetting himself. He shrank back meekly at Gregory's scowl.

Gregory shoved a bowl of stew at him. "Eat, then get back out to stables."

"Yessir." Cuthbert managed to make the stew – which was comprised of unidentifiable shreds of meat and gristle, and the sort of vegetation traditionally found in the poorest peasant fare – disappear with a speed that a wolf might have envied.

Chaucer ate half of his own food then shoved the rest towards Cuthbert. "He looks like he needs it," he said, when Gregory looked at him askance.

The knight couldn't really argue with that. Cuthbert looked a lot healthier than he had two weeks ago but that wasn't saying much. Examining the poet, Gregory realised that Chaucer wasn't as old as he'd thought. Perhaps late in his third decade, only ten years older than Gregory himself. Chaucer had used the water and cloth provided by the tavern girl to sponge off most of the grime and blood. The bruises were ugly but not serious and the head wound appeared superficial. He'd live.

"I may be able to repay you for your assistance," Chaucer said, after he'd arranged for a message to be sent to his house in Aldgate.

"Really?" Gregory was aware his tone was defensive and it made him surlier than ever.

"Is your servant finished? I fear he may be about to fall asleep in his bowl."

Gregory saw that Cuthbert was indeed nodding off, worn out with excitement and a full belly. He shook the boy gently. "Off with you."

"Yes...my...lord." Cuthbert's words formed around a huge yawn. He trotted blearily off in the direction of the stables.

"No argument for change." Gregory looked up to find Chaucer regarding him with interest. "Is something amiss, Master Chaucer?"

"Do you usually allow your servants to argue with you, Sir Maudesley?"

"Of course not. But nothing makes an impression on young Cuthbert for long."

Chaucer did not appear satisfied with this as an explanation. "You speak more like the boy's guardian."

"I speak like someone who paid a good shilling for that boy. There's no point starving a servant if you want them to work off what you paid for them," Gregory said, his tone forbidding further comment. "And you can thank Cuthbert for your precious messages, if not your life, Master Chaucer." Gregory nodded to the poet's script. "If it had been left to me, I'd have stayed here with my ale, not gone tearing off into the night to help a man who spouted poetry at me while I lay in a…" He broke off, annoyed with himself for saying so much.

"I quite understand," Chaucer replied. "You are a man of action, fresh from some war or another. What need have you for courtesy or compassion? Let other knights cling to such foibles." Chaucer smiled in that dry way of his and Gregory finally laid a finger on what annoyed him about the man – he could never tell if Chaucer was mocking him or not.

"And yet," the poet went on, "you *did* go tearing out into the night, rushing to the aid of a man you do not especially like…"

"I didn't know it was you until the fight was over."

"…at the behest of your young servant. A scrap of a youth, who nevertheless seems to believe you are all the knights of the round table rolled into one. But certainly it is because the lad cost you a shilling and not from any nobler concerns." Chaucer looked slyly pleased with himself and Gregory half wished he'd left him in the alley.

"Nobler concerns are luxuries a man like me cannot afford," Gregory said. "Was there some other business you had with me, Master Chaucer?"

"You said you were not a baronet yet. But you expect to be?"

"If the king will ever deign to accept my oath of homage," Gregory said.

"And you've been kept waiting by that imbecile, Foxworth, I expect. The seneschal, I mean," Chaucer said.

Gregory nodded.

"Have you heard of me, Sir Maudesley? Don't imagine I seek to flatter my vanity. I only wish to know whether you will believe me when I say that I am well connected at the palace."

"One poet is much like another to me. I've no taste for the…the art." Gregory managed to substitute the word he'd been going to use at the last moment.

Chaucer's shrewd, dark eyes gleamed, undeceived and apparently unoffended. "I am not merely a poet. I am many other things. Perhaps the most useful of these to you, is my role as clerk at the Savoy Palace."

"Speak plain, Master Chaucer. What are you saying?"

"I'm saying that if you will meet me at the Savoy Palace tomorrow, I believe I can arrange an audience for you with the king. It won't strictly be following protocol but I don't much care for Foxworth's petty tyranny over supplicants. The man considers himself far more important than he is." Chaucer's mouth twisted in disdain.

Gregory scarcely heard a word after 'audience with the king'. To no longer be stuck in the city. To finally get the wretched business of his inheritance settled and make his way home. Why, if Chaucer was as good as his word, he and Cuthbert might be on their way back to Wynnstree late tomorrow. They would be well away before the rebels decided what they intended to do now they'd reached London. No need to get caught up in the ugly business of a rebellion.

"The king has gone to the Tower. They'll not let anyone in to see him," Gregory said.

Chaucer pushed his hat back on his head. "They will let me in and you with me, if I vouch for you."

"Then I will meet you tomorrow." Gregory forced himself to frame a few words of gratitude. "You have my thanks, Master Chaucer." He couldn't stop himself nodding to the script, "those messages must have been worth a great deal."

Chaucer laughed, a full rich sound, less ragged than his laughter in the alley. "You don't think I carry messages on paper, Maudesley, do you?"

"What were you in such a fever to save your bag for then?" Gregory scowled.

"My work, of course. My newest set of verses, still very raw and unpolished, but gems nevertheless."

"I waded into a knife fight to save some bloody poetry? God's Wounds," Gregory said, in disbelief.

"And my life, incidentally," Chaucer said drily. "My work and my life, two things I do not hold to be mere trifles." He rose. "Besides, I believe you entered that brawl for your own reasons as much as mine, but an obligation is an obligation. I will see you on the morrow."

He clapped Gregory on the shoulder and went to where a very large man servant was waiting by the inn door. Evidently the message he'd sent home earlier had yielded results. Gregory went to his own bed, reflecting that cultivating a friendship with Chaucer was not the worst idea in the world. Anyone who could see the king more or less on demand was worth knowing.

10.

13th June, 1381

The Strand with its Thames side access and river view houses, was one of the wealthiest and most exclusive districts in London. Here, in the multi-storey dwellings, built of the finest stone and timber with leaded roofs and decorative crenellations, dwelt the nobility – the cream of London society. The road was paved, rather than packed dirt, and Drum's hooves rang out against the stones. It was a muggy day. The pressured heat promising early storms and frayed tempers, but the breeze blowing off the river was cool and fresh.

"Nowhere in this whole stinking city smells this good," Cuthbert muttered with unaccustomed dolor. "This isn't meant for the likes of me."

Gregory glanced at the boy, wondering if he should have left him at the inn. Cuthbert was riding Patience, both of them out of place on this clean and shining street. "You're my servant so you belong here if I say you do."

"Yes, my lord," Cuthbert replied doubtfully.

Truthfully, the opulent houses and obvious wealth were making Gregory uncomfortable. He was only a country knight, not even a baronet yet. Refurbishing his wardrobe had not been at the top of his list of priorities when scratching around for enough cash to pay his inheritance relief, and it showed. It occurred to Gregory that had William been in his place, his brother's careless charm and confidence would have carried the day. Gregory was all too aware of being insufficient, which meant his temper was closer to the surface than usual. Drum, being a very fine warhorse, was the only one of the quartet who did not present a jarring contrast to the surroundings.

It was not merely being out of place that had Gregory tensing as if an unseen archer had a crossbow sight pointed between his shoulder blades. London felt like a pot about to boil over. The hostility and subdued fury he'd encountered on his way to the city had trickled in after him. Whispers had become shouts. A call to arms might come any moment now, not from the king or his counsel, but from the surrounding countryside. London stood ready to answer and there would be hell to pay if she did.

Gregory had experienced this sense of unease before. It always preceded a sudden need for departure. In the end he had not dared to leave Cuthbert or any of his possessions in *the Half Moon,* lest he be cut off from them by the rising tide of rebellion.

Cuthbert shifted in his saddle, swiping sweat off his forehead as the mare lashed her tail at small, irritating flies. "I think there's a storm coming, my lord."

You might just be right there, Gregory thought.

They arrived at the Savoy Palace and Gregory had difficulty keeping his customary scowl in place. It was the London residence of John of Gaunt, Duke of Lancaster and uncle to the king. It was the prize jewel in the strong box of the Strand. A huge, sprawling pile, of which every stone and limewashed beam spoke of wealth, and the power that goes with it. The walls were crenelated like battlements, and the gables had 'corbie-steps' which Gregory had only seen in the cities of France and Italy before. The plaster, where its use was necessary, had been painted a light golden brown which caught the reflected morning light from the river, making the building appear to shimmer.

"I can't wait out here with the horses," Cuthbert said, in a tone of high tragedy. "I'll get taken up for loitering."

"Don't be ridiculous," Gregory snapped. "You'll not be waiting on the street. There are stables."

Cuthbert gave Gregory a hangdog look full of reproach but fell in beside him without a murmur as they made their way around the side of the palace. All the while, Gregory's unease grew. He understood Cuthbert's desire to get away from here. For all the splendour of the palace, it felt increasingly like a trap.

"If anything unusual happens, anything at all, you're to take Drum and that wretched mare, and get away from here."

"But what about you, my lord?"

"I'll move a lot faster if I don't have concern myself with you," Gregory said. "And no cheating on my orders this time, or I'll give you a thrashing that'll make you remember your previous master fondly."

Cuthbert's mouth curled mulishly. "I'll take the horses away, my lord. Just as you said."

***

Chaucer looked up from the document he was reading and Gregory saw the poet wore a grim expression. The bruises looked appalling by daylight. Superficial injuries but dark and damning against the pallor of his narrow, clever face. "Sir Maudesley, well met."

"Master Chaucer. How's the head wound?" Gregory said.

"Did you see any disturbances on your way here?"

"The streets were quiet." Gregory realised the poet knew what that meant. A city the size of London with few folk abroad and little business being conducted? Animals were said to know when a storm would hit, weren't they? "You think people are hiding indoors?"

"I think we'd better engage an escort to the Tower, and be quick about it," Chaucer said. "I've had word that a party of Kentish rebels numbering in the thousands has camped at Blackheath. What does that suggest to you, Maudesley?"

"With the Essex insurgents on the other side of the Thames, a pincer manoeuvre," Gregory said. "It's no mere gang of malcontents. They're organised." It was going to be worse than that long ago bread riot. Much worse.

"Come, Sir Maudesley," Chaucer reached for the door only to be nearly taken off his feet by the frightened page who threw it open.

"What in God's name—"

"They're coming!" The boy gasped. "The rebels!"

"Where?" Gregory grabbed the page, giving him a little shake. "How close are they?"

73

"They're...they're here," the boy quavered. "The guards just opened the gates for them."

Raised voices in the hallway were followed by what sounded like glass shattering.

The rebels had entered London and headed straight for the wealthiest areas. They'd come for the instigators of their woes. First among them, the hated lord and man of state, John of Gaunt. Creator of the poll tax that had seen Bampton's clerks slaughtered at Brentwood.

Gregory kept one hand tight on the page's shoulder. The boy's frightened gaze skittered around the room, a trapped animal seeking escape. "Is His Grace home?"

"No," Chaucer said. "You think they mean harm to his person?"

"If they do, they're out of luck. And they'll be looking for alternatives."

Chaucer paled further under his bruises. He'd no doubt heard all about Brentwood's staff. "But...the guards. They can't just march into His Grace's residence unchallenged."

Gregory recognised the belief in the poet's eyes. The man was no fool but caught by surprise he had the fox's urge to run to earth, even though the way was snared, even though the hounds were on his tail and would dig him out. "Doesn't matter what they can do when they've already done it. Does His Grace have enough men-at-arms to dissuade a few thousand furious rebels who believe that God and right are on their side?"

Chaucer's mouth trembled. "No one has enough guards for that."

Another crash came from outside the clerks' office. The rebels would be there soon.

"Is there another way out of here?" Gregory said.

Chaucer shook his head.

"Then we leave through the door." Gregory gave the now sobbing page another little shake. "Enough, they're not likely to be after boys and servants." He met Chaucer's gaze. There was no need to voice what they were both thinking: the rebels might very well be looking for clerks.

The poet snatched the velvet cap from his head and tossed it onto a desk. He tugged at the laces of his sleeves and in a moment his tastefully embroidered cote-hardie joined the cap. "Best I do not look to be obviously part of the Duke's household."

Gregory had to agree. In his doublet and stockings – both of plain, well-made cloth – Chaucer might pass for a man servant. At first glance at least. Gregory opened the door carefully and looked out. The hallway was clear. Whatever the rebels had found a few rooms back was keeping them occupied.

"Master Chaucer, which is the best way out of the palace?"

"This way." Chaucer edged past Gregory into the hall, and took the lead. The page followed and Gregory brought up the rear. Of the three of them he was perhaps the most likely to be challenged, but he was also the mostly likely to be able to fend off an attack.

Another crash came from behind them, followed by the roar of voices raised in furious exultation. The page's nerve broke. He ducked away from Gregory, nimbly nipped past Chaucer and took to his heels.

"Wait–" Chaucer began but the lad was gone. "I cannot help but believe that boy has the right idea."

Gregory chuckled. The unease had passed. Now that he was taking action, now that the storm had arrived, there was no dread. No confusion. His heart beat fast with exhilaration not fear. They turned onto another seemingly endless corridor. "How much further?"

"A good step," Chaucer said sourly. "I could be forgiven for thinking you're enjoying yourself, Maudesley."

Gregory was spared the effort of a reply, when a party of men spilled out of a doorway on his left.

"Halt! State your business!" the ringleader cried, with what Gregory considered to be breath-taking impudence.

"Be easy, sirrah," Chaucer said, lifting his hands in a placating gesture.

"We're nothing to do with His Grace so stand aside and we'll be on our way," Gregory said. Every nerve sang. His hand twitched in the direction of his sword. "We don't want any trouble."

"You don't sound the slightest bit convincing," Chaucer muttered.

The leader eyed Gregory's cloak and clearly took him for what he was, despite his scruffy appearance. "Hand over that pig sticker and we'll think about it."

His companions laughed.

"Bollocks to that," Gregory said and backhanded the man out of his way.

It might still have worked out in his favour. Gregory was a huge man, strong and fast, trained to combat and very experienced. Then again, anyone can be felled by a well-placed blow, and Gregory had forgotten about the doorway opposite. He didn't see the figure lurking out of sight inside. Nor did he see the gleaming, solid silver candlestick describe a graceful, shining arc through the air as the hidden man brought it crashing down on Gregory's head.

There was a sudden, high pitched ringing in his left ear. Brilliant green and orange sparks erupted behind his eyes. The world went white. And then black.

11.

2nd — 19th May, 1361
Four weeks earlier

Gregory woke the morning after the wedding to discover Alienor had already left. He found her, after much searching, engaged in conversation with the under-steward in the buttery. She frowned when she saw him and turned away. Her actions irritated him but Gregory had other matters that required his attention, so he left his new wife to her own devices. Two weeks before the rest of the dowry would be his, the baron had said. Gregory chafed at the delay, biting back his temper and frightening his remaining servants with his curt orders and dark scowls. He and Fletcher rode out to inspect the state of his farmland and flocks, to see how many villeins by land were left. There had been precious few villeins by blood even before the sickness. Those who remained, numbered a mere handful. With little chance of offering competitive wages, this year's harvest was already looking bleak.

The days took on a pattern. He would wake, find his wife already gone about her day, follow Fletcher on the latest tour of disaster or avoid looking at increasingly depressing lists of accounts. Finally, he would see Alienor at dinner, where there would be indifferent food and silence, before bed, where he told her to put out the light and go to sleep. Alienor never asked him why he had not yet claimed his marital rights, but sometimes he would catch her just turning her head as if she had been looking at him a moment before, a slight frown on her face.

Gregory was finding the presence of a wife something of a trial. He was still in the process of mentally reclaiming his family's castle, which had not really been home since he was a lad of twelve. There had been visits of course. When Gregory had served as a squire, his knight master had found Maudesley

77

Castle a convenient stopping place on the way to London. But it was always understood that the castle, the grounds, the farms and the lands were intended for William.

It was William whom Gregory resentfully mourned, and William whom he blamed for his current troubles. He would find odd memories tucked in forgotten corners of the castle. On turning a mundane corner to an unused chamber, it would be a boyish William who greeted Gregory from his memory, reminding him how he'd worshipped his older brother. In the tangled thicket of the orchard, it was an older, taunting William who laughed from the branches of an apple tree. There were things Gregory had thought forgotten forever and memories he wished were indeed lost. It was more painful than pleasant. He'd thought he'd made his peace with it all, left it behind him when he went to fight for strangers in foreign lands. It made him morose and short tempered, dwelling on dark thoughts and hating his brother for everything he'd done. For everything he, Gregory, had to do in order to inherit what he had deserved so much more than William ever had.

But now, everywhere Gregory turned, he found William's ghost competing with Alienor's presence. She didn't even have to be in the room, he discovered to his annoyance. It started with small changes. The reorganising of a room, the airing of linens. Then a chamber off the kitchens was converted into a still room. The kitchen garden was dug over and freshly planted – with what Gregory wasn't sure. For all he knew his wife was growing monkshood and nightshade – a disconcerting thought. The kitchens followed in Alienor's program of reorganisation and improvement. Consequently the food that emerged was of a better standard, even though the same ingredients went into preparing it. Gregory found himself in a constant state of pique. He hadn't asked her to make improvements. What did she think she was about? As slowly but surely Alienor's influence moved through the castle, it fell to her control, one piece at a time. Formerly directionless and impervious servants became quick and competent. Everything was clean. Maudesley Castle stopped looking like a grim and desolate seat and more like a lord's home. She permeated everything, like mist or perfume.

And Gregory couldn't fathom how his wife was accomplishing so much, because as far as he could see, she spent no coin on improvements and he never actually saw her do anything.

Fletcher's wiry white eyebrows rose when Gregory finally voiced his concerns. "Are you not pleased that the household is responding to her?"

"What? Yes…of course…" Gregory trailed off, unable to put into words how uncomfortable her actions were making him. What was he to say? That he did not expect her to act the part of lady of the house? "She's just…everywhere," he fumbled. "The castle will be more hers than mine at this rate."

Fletcher eyed him sidelong. "Well, the lady has a sharp enough tongue, it's true. Many a servant has felt the keen edge of it since she came here. But for all that, it would seem Lady Alienor is improving matters. She has a skill for household management that I lack, my lord."

"The household was fine under your guidance," Gregory grumbled. "Why she should concern herself down to the level of kitchen scuts and gardeners? Has she nothing else to do?"

Fletcher stared carefully ahead between the ears of his ancient grey mare. "Did you expect her to occupy herself with stitching altar cloths, my lord?"

Gregory gritted his teeth, ignoring the dull heat rising in his face. He *had* expected that. He had expected to provide a home for a wealthy but unsuitable woman, take possession of her dowry and have her be grateful enough to keep out of his way. He had not expected to be constantly reminded of her presence. Dining with her of an evening, in addition to providing her with a home, had seemed to him to be all that could be expected of him, given her stained reputation.

Fletcher cleared his throat.

"What is it?" Gregory snapped.

"My lord, forgive me. But given the circumstances of your courtship, I could not help wondering whether you have asked Lady Alienor about her…her misdemeanour."

"Why in God's name would I do that?" Gregory's temper strained against its bonds.

"To hear the truth of the matter, my lord." Fletcher's tone was without inflection.

"The truth," Gregory scoffed. "I'm not likely to hear that from her. But I'll have it one way or another in a few months' time."

Fletcher was quiet for a moment. "I see."

"Do you?" Gregory kicked his horse into a trot, forcing Fletcher to keep up. "I didn't ask you for marital advice. You forget yourself."

"Yes, my lord."

Fletcher's meekness irritated Gregory even further. He held his tongue for a mile or so, then finally said, "You believe I should speak to her?"

"I believe only that you might find the truth somewhat different than we have been led to believe. Rumour cares nothing for veracity after all, my lord."

"She herself said the rumour was correct," Gregory said.

Fletcher shook his head. "Lady Alienor made sure all her suitors knew of the rumours, certainly. But if I recall correctly, and admittedly I am old now and my memory does not retain facts so well as it once did, the lady did not actually say she was guilty of the charges laid against her."

"Then why didn't someone else marry her?" Gregory demanded. "With what the baron paid me…*will* pay me, she would have been a highly desirable bride."

"The baron believed his niece to be guilty," Fletcher said. "No doubt that and the lady's frankness weighed with many a suitor. Perhaps she frightened off others with her acidic tongue."

"Weaklings," Gregory snorted, although he too went in some apprehension of Alienor's talent for finding a man's weakness, then revealing it to the world.

"The point," Fletcher said, "is that she accepted you, when she refused or repelled many others."

Gregory slowed his horse to a walk and stared at his steward. "If you're suggesting the girl *likes* me, I can assure you you're mistaken."

"I didn't say that she liked you, my lord. Only that she might be willing to." Fletcher shrugged. "Life is a lot more pleasant when your wife is your ally."

Gregory thought over Fletcher's words before finally dismissing them. It made no sense that Alienor had married an impoverished baronet of uncertain temper, without even a pleasing manner, court polish or fine looks to recommend him to a lady. Not if she really was innocent. Why should she have chosen him over the others? Gregory was a large, powerful man but blocky and unlovely. Fine for warfare but of limited use elsewhere. Alienor was damnably clever. Gregory was no fool and had been educated alongside William, but he had never excelled. He had no refinement. No appreciation for the arts. Nothing in common with his quick witted wife. Only desperation could have led Alienor to accept him. Being the best of a poor selection wasn't much consolation. And why should he care about his wife's preferences? There could only be one master of Maudesley Castle. He'd see that Alienor understood that. And she could just cultivate a little gratitude that he was willing to rear her bastard when it arrived.

Gregory realised Fletcher was still speaking and cut him off. "I'll thank you hold back any further opinions of my wife. You forget yourself, Fletcher."

Fletcher's jaw hardened, the lines deepening around his mouth. "Yes, my lord."

They rode on in silence.

Gregory sought Alienor out that evening, determined to impress upon her just who was in charge. He had not returned in time to dine with the household and she had once again been absent when he woke. She was not to be easily tracked down. He tried the kitchens, the still room, the garden. He went out onto the curtain wall, where he knew she liked to walk. His wife was nowhere to be found and he couldn't bring himself to enquire her whereabouts of his servants or have one of them seek her out. Growing increasingly irritated, because the girl had embedded herself like a briar in the fabric of the household, Gregory finally happened upon her in the room which had served as his father's study.

Alienor was sitting in a chair before the fire – which she'd obviously had lit because no one else ever came into this room – poring over a sheaf of papers. She looked up, clearly surprised to see him. "My lord," she said with frosty politeness, "what brings you here?"

Fury travelled up Gregory's spine in a flashfire that left him unable to form words for a moment. "I might ask you the same question, my lady." He strove for the same indifferent courtesy she had shown him. And failed.

Alienor's eyes glinted. She knew she had annoyed him and it pleased her. "My reasons for being here are twofold. I thought to put these papers and accounts in order. And I was...rationing myself on the pleasure of your company. It's too rich a meal for every day consumption."

"You thought shutting yourself up with a lot of dusty old books and papers was an adequate hiding place, did you?" Gregory chose not to mention the half hour he had spent looking for her.

Alienor canted her head to one side, as if considering his words. "It was clear to me that this was one place you never frequented. You do not read much or take pleasure in this side of running your estate, do you, my lord?"

"I am not yet able to run my estate because your guardian has not delivered what he promised," Gregory snapped.

Alienor's mouth hardened. "I'm all too aware your only interest in me was my dowry, my lord. It's discourteous to bring it up so often."

Gregory found he disliked her gentle reproof even more than her continual needling. "Am I not keeping my side of the bargain? Besides, you've certainly made yourself at home. A little over a fortnight and you've already rearranged half the castle."

Alienor gave him a look which could only be described as deep pity for immeasurable stupidity. "What else should I be doing, my lord? As your wife, is it not my place to rule your household and see to its efficient running, as it is your place to rule your lands?"

Gregory opened his mouth but found that once again, he could not form an argument against her.

Alienor went on, tone sharp. "Is it merely my presence which offends you, my lord? Or is it, that as undesirable a wife as I

82

might be, you are irritated at my having more use than merely being a source of some easily accessible coin?"

"I am the lord of this demesne." This was not going how Gregory had expected.

"And as your wife, it is my duty to be your helpmeet," Alienor said. "Or have you deemed that that is yet another wifely duty I am unfit to perform?"

Gregory found that the study had suddenly become uncomfortably hot and close.

Alienor took a breath and spoke less sharply. "I've been through the accounts. Your father kept good records until his final sickness. They were just somewhat out of order. It's not good news exactly. But it may not be as dire as you fear. I have suggestions I think will help. Will you take a look, my lord?"

She offered him the scrap of parchment almost shyly. Gregory took it on reflex, aware of the pulsing blood in his temples, of the tightness around his ribs, the beads of sweat forming at the nape of his neck. He glanced at the neat, finely written script – a list of expenditures and notes next to a column of amounts. And that was all he could discern before the words started swimming across the page, twisting back on themselves nonsensically. Alienor's clear writing tied itself into knots which he could have untangled with time and patience, but not then, not while he was under her gaze.

Alienor was standing far closer to Gregory than he thought necessary. She was speaking but he couldn't concentrate on the words. There was just the gentle rise and fall of her voice, a musical cadence that drained sense from what she was saying as surely as written word drained sense from fact. Her hand reached across the paper, one long, slender finger tracing a column as she explained her idea. Her hair smelled of some sort of flowers and her warmth burned into him. None of it made any sense. The words on the page were as inscrutable as her motives.

"My lord? Have I lost your attention?" Alienor actually laughed a little.

Gregory remembered how surprised she'd been to see him here in the study. The sneer stung afresh. This was all to make him appear foolish. More of her games, when all the while she scorned him as an oaf and thought him little more intelligent than a block of wood.

Gregory's fingers curled, the paper crumpling in one huge hand. He pushed away from his wife, glaring. "This is not your business, Madam."

Alienor stared at him. He thought he saw a flash of hurt in her grey eyes before they froze over. "Someone needs to suggest something," she said coldly. "You cannot do all yourself, my lord. Surely you are strategist enough to see that?"

"What concern is it of yours?" Gregory demanded.

"It is very much my concern since this is now my home and will be my children's home... If we ever have any," Alienor said.

"Interesting that you should choose that as your argument," Gregory said, beyond embarrassment and attraction, and now in the comforting hinterlands of anger once more. "You need have no fear I will not provide for you. And your bastard too, when it makes an appearance."

Alienor's eyes snapped with sudden fury. "My *what*? Of what child can you be speaking, my lord? I would ask if I'd missed an important event whilst slumbering, except surely that is not how you will refer to your own child?"

Gregory swept a pile of books and papers off the desk with sudden, violent swipe of his arm. "You were carrying a child when we wed," he accused.

"Who has told you such a thing?"

"I am not a fool."

"I cannot agree with that assessment."

"Why else would you... The circumstances. Your reputation. Even your guardian believes your virtue cast aside," Gregory said.

Alienor gave him a look of disgust. "My guardian made up his own mind without asking me for the truth. My father would have been worse. But I despise lies and will not tell them. I am not with child. I never have been."

"But...?"

"My lord, I know little of such matters having no experience of them, but as I understand it, in order to get with child, a lass must couple with a man. Or does your greater experience of the world say me false?" Alienor was now white with rage.

"And yet you married me in such haste," Gregory pointed out, trying for a reasonable tone despite the whirling of his thoughts. Could Fletcher have been right?

"What do you imagine my alternatives were?" Alienor said. "Here is the story since you will not ask. I come from a large family. My brothers and sisters were all much older than me. I was the last child of Laird Douglas and his lady, and left much on my own."

It didn't occur to Gregory to try to silence her. He was transfixed, fascinated by her rage rather than repelled by it. God help him if that was how matters stood.

"We had blood villeins in the West March too. And no one ever told me I should not play with the villeins' children. Who would do so? My father was always occupied with border disputes. The villeins could not tell a daughter of Laird Douglas what she might do or no, and so I came to befriend a lad my own age. A villein's son. We grew up together and he was closer to me than any brother. My dearest friend. When a false accusation was made against him, I helped him to break his bond and run away, rather than hang for a crime he did not commit."

Gregory was not especially pleased to hear that his wife had helped a villein to escape his lord – her own father, come to that. He was even less enamoured with the idea that there was a man out there somewhere who had such a claim on his wife's affections. "What possible relevance can this have to your stained virtue?"

"My virtue is not stained!" Alienor's lip curled, showing small, sharp, white teeth. "I suppose you might accuse me of theft since the villein was my father's property, but I helped him escape because it was right. If he could stay free for a year and a day, then he'd be a free man, not a villein. He could be tried justly, if he chose. Or find work elsewhere."

Gregory did not bother to correct her. It was a popular belief that blood villeinage could be broken in such a way. In truth it depended greatly on the villein's cheated master. He'd heard of one mesne lord who'd pursued a runaway villein for twenty years.

"And so for my waywardness, I was banished to my uncle's lands, allowing my father's temper to cool. The lad I helped free heard what had become of me. He came to see that I was well and had not been harmed for helping him. I met him in the stables in secret because I would not have him caught and returned to my father. When we were saying farewell, my uncle's head groom came upon us and misconstrued what he saw." Alienor lifted her chin. "There was no one to take my side, save Mairi, and who believes a maid of the chamber if they will not listen to the lady?"

"And then?" Gregory said, annoyed with himself. What did it matter? He'd married her as a business arrangement. He'd needed her dowry. She'd needed his good name. A simple transaction. And yet he was unable to tear himself free of her tale.

"Then my uncle was in a fury," Alienor said drily. "But his temper cools faster than Laird Douglas's and my mother was his favourite sister. My uncle would do much for me for her sake. Besides, my father wanted me to find a husband and provided an appropriate sum to induce the right suitor. My uncle did not want to admit his laxity as a guardian to my father. He reasoned, much as you did, that any unfortunate results of my presumed dalliance must be concealed with a marriage."

"Yet you never denied these accusations?" Gregory realised he wanted it to be true, perhaps from pride or vanity, or some other inexplicable reason. He could not trust his judgement on the matter.

"I denied them heartily. No one heeded me at all," Alienor said bitterly.

"This is... It's a tale fit for a minstrel," Gregory said. "I cannot believe it. What is the name of this villein you claim to have aided?"

Alienor's eyes grew cold. "You must think me a fool if you believe I would give him up after all my trouble. What would you do with him? Send him back to the Marches? Or make him swear he did not take my maidenhead? Why should a man's word hold more truth than mine?"

"You expect me to believe this is true, yet you did not tell me before." He disliked how easily she had seen through him.

"You led me to believe that it did not matter to you, and you married me without ever asking for my tale. I'd no notion it weighed upon you, until you started speaking of bastards," Alienor said, thoroughly exasperated. "I've done nothing I'm ashamed of. And I'm sorely to be pitied, because having sorted through the petty nobility of three counties on pains that I must marry one of them, I still managed to yoke myself to a fool."

"You will address me with more respect, girl," Gregory snapped.

"I beg your pardon – you're a fool, *my lord*." Alienor swept past him like a queen, turning at the door to point to the paper still crumpled in his hand. "And you're even more a fool if you don't at least consider my suggestions."

"Come back here!"

"I think not, my lord," Alienor said. "Tell me, is it that you will not read what I've written? Or that you cannot?"

"Of course I can read," Gregory snapped.

"A shame. Ignorance can be remedied whereas wilful ignorance cannot."

Gregory was dimly aware that he should not allow her to leave. That if she did, she would have won this battle. "Alienor." He thought it might be the first time he'd used her name. She paused halfway through the door. "I don't know what to believe."

"Oh that's easy enough, my lord," she said. "Wait nine moons and you'll have an answer. That was your plan, no?"

Gregory said nothing.

"Much becomes clear," Alienor said. "And with that in mind, I'm sure there are other beds in the castle that will welcome your presence more than I do."

The door closed hard behind her and this time, Gregory didn't call her back.

12.

13th June, 1381

Gregory awoke to blurred and distant laughter. He blinked, half expecting the sun to cut into his eyes because he had the most God awful hangover and… It came back to him in a rush. He sat upright and groaned.

"Ah, the noble knight is back. Excellent." Chaucer's voice dripped sarcasm.

Gregory held his head, squinting in an attempt to make the room stop the slow, lazy revolutions it was currently looping around him. "What happened?"

"What happened? You, paragon of the knightly code, caught the scent of blood and threw our escape plan out on the midden," the poet fumed. "Your head is harder than an anvil, by the by, which I suppose explains your bull headed approach to communication."

"I never claimed to be a diplomat." Gregory rubbed the side of his skull, wincing at the lump rising under his hair. It was the second time inside a month that he'd been knocked unconscious. "Where are we?" He peered into the gloom. The air was still and musty. There was an earthy scent and something like aged wood. A faint, rich, wine smell. And something else. A thread of something far more alarming. If only he could think straight. "It feels like we're underground."

"That's because we're locked in His Grace's cellars," Chaucer said. "And some fast talking I had to do to get us here too."

"Weren't we supposed to be getting out of the palace?" Gregory said. "What bloody good is it to be shut up in the cellar?"

"Those rebels we happened upon were all for killing you after you showed your true colours. They took it for support of the

Duke. They were all for killing me too, though fortunately they didn't realise I'm a clerk."

"Instead we're both alive but trapped in the cellar." Gregory could see that it was an improvement over being dead, although not by much.

"The *wine* cellar," Chaucer stressed the word. "I traded His Grace's finest vintages for our miserable hides."

Gregory was torn between amusement and dismay. On one hand, Chaucer was quite the fox to have thought of it so quickly, and it explained the drunken laughter he could hear coming from the other end of the cellars. On the other, he sincerely hoped word of this never reached John of Gaunt. Gregory doubted the Duke of Lancaster would consider the trade worthwhile.

"So when they've all had a skin full, the second part of the plan is to do what exactly?" The knight flexed his hands and rolled his shoulders. The pain in his head was huge but he could work around it.

"I suppose hoping they would all drink themselves unconscious, so we could sneak past them, was too much to ask for," Chaucer said. "This is a lesser chamber in the cellars. They've barred the door to keep us here. But there might be another way out. The barrels of wine and crates of goods are brought up from His Grace's private dock."

Gregory pursed his lips. "And you know where this other way out is?"

"I have a theory," Chaucer said.

Gregory caught a faint whiff of the scent which had sparked alarm before. It was stronger now, or he was more in his wits to appreciate it. "It's a time to have a certainty. I can smell burning."

"Oh yes," Chaucer said, his tone eerily calm. "The rebels have set fire to the palace."

Gregory swore and leapt to his feet. There was no time to be alarmed at how unsteady his legs were. No time to double over and puke his tripes up, like he half wanted to. "Help me!" he snarled at the poet, in between cursing one saint's testicles and feeling along the rough brick walls in the dim light. There were crates and barrels and rolls of waxed cloth stacked everywhere. Gregory sent several crashing to the ground as he cleared the walls.

Nothing and nothing and no way out.

Was it his imagination or had it grown warmer? "Damn it, help me, you prancing fool!"

But Chaucer had already made his way to another stack of crates and barrels. "Here, Maudesley. Do you feel it?" He was holding his hand palm out to a tiny gap in the stacked goods.

Gregory crossed the cellar in three strides. "What in hell's name are you–" He broke off. A cool draught whistling faintly between the crates.

"I thought I might have found it before you woke," Chaucer explained. "But it was fainter then. I could not be sure."

The cellar was definitely growing warmer. The air coming from whatever was behind the crates felt wintry by comparison. Gregory yanked at one crate. It scraped across the floor a mere inch. They were half as tall as him and stacked three deep and two high. The barrels were smaller but scarcely any lighter. No wonder Chaucer had waited for him to come round. The smaller man could not have moved them by himself. Gregory set his strength and weight against the crate, hooking his fingers under the lip of the lid and pulling.

Chaucer joined him and between them they shoved it against the opposite wall. They started on the next one. It was slow going. Sweat trickled down Gregory's spine, welding skin and shirt together. It fell stinging into his eyes. He tipped barrels on their sides and Chaucer rolled them away.

By the time they'd reached the last layer of crates, Gregory's head was banging like a barn door in a high wind. His vision kept doubling. The air was so hot, breathing was like inhaling banked coals. His skin felt dry and tight, shrinking back as if to cling to his skull. No sweat now, just hideous heat and short, laboured breaths that provided no relief.

"That should...be...big...enough..." Chaucer panted.

They'd cleared a gap all the way to the wall and the poet obviously expected to find a tunnel that would lead down to the dock. But when he squeezed between the remaining stacked crates, he came to a sudden swearing halt.

"What is it?" Gregory felt light headed. The world kept slipping sideways, then righting itself. The air was turning bad. An idle part of his mind considered irrelevantly how calm and composed the poet had been up until that moment. A man of many talents. One used to danger and the quick exercise of his wits. A king's man...

The stinging blow across his face made Gregory blink stupidly at Chaucer. He'd been on the verge of passing out.

"Do not go to sleep, Maudesley!" Chaucer snapped. "It took three men to carry you down here and all of them were bigger than me."

"I'm...the air..." Gregory said groggily.

"It's turning foul," Chaucer said grimly. "Hardly any smoke. That's bad, Maudesley. This part of the cellars must be under part of the palace that is even now merrily burning to ash. We shall be next if you do not put yourself in your wits."

"Yes...yes, alright..."

"There's an ironwork gate across the tunnel." Chaucer swallowed. "It's locked."

"Need a key then..." Gregory fought to concentrate but the poet's words came now fuzzy and loud, now muted and soft.

"We'll make a scholar of you yet with that ability to reason," Chaucer said acidly. He slapped Gregory's face again. "We have no key."

"Let me see..." Gregory pushed past the smaller man, shouldering his way between the crates and barrels. "You're right. There is a gate..." He thought he could hear the poet cursing, knocking something over, then swearing again in a different tone.

He stared at the gate, trying to make sense of it. Thin bars of iron riveted diagonally across each other to leave small diamond shaped gaps. The top of the gate was a series of sharp spikes resting against the tunnel lintel. The lock looked depressingly secure. They really should wait for someone to come along with a key. Gregory knew he could break down a door as long as it wasn't too thick, but not an iron gate. He'd only break a shoulder trying. Besides, even if this was a wooden door, it opened towards him. So any attempt to break it down meant that he'd be trying to tear the lock free in the direction it was most secure.

Gregory paused, frowning. That was important somehow. Wasn't it? It was too hot to think. And his head hurt. He wanted to close his eyes, sleep a little. Try again when the air was cooler. A bowel loosening crash came from directly overhead and Gregory snapped his eyes open, the sudden cold wash of fear through his veins compensating temporarily for the lack of air.

"Maudesley I swear to God if you've died in there and blocked our escape route, I will seek you out in the afterlife and geld you!" Chaucer cried. "The ceiling will not hold much longer. The palace is collapsing."

The roof was caving in. They wouldn't burn to death after all.

The palace was *collapsing*.

They would be buried alive in in the smouldering remains.

A breath of cold, river sweet air whispered through a gap in the grill and suddenly Gregory understood what he was looking at. He couldn't unlock the gate. He couldn't break it down. But he could lift it off its hinges.

Gregory bent his knees, trying to get his hips under the weight of the gate, getting as good a grip as he could manage on the bars. He heaved. There was a hideous squeal of protesting metal and the gate inched upward. Gregory shifted his hips under the weight, stopping the gate from sliding back into place. He adjusted his hands and heaved again. The gate screamed as if it was being tortured. Something pinged at the base of Gregory's spine, the bars cut into his hands. They were hot. Not burning, not yet, but too hot to hold comfortably. His heart went from a canter to a gallop and he threw all his strength into a final, desperate shove. Metal squealed and the hinges kissed the tips of the pins. An endless moment of shaking strain where the gate would go no further because the lock had bent and warped, preventing the hinges coming free. And then something snapped and Gregory was falling backwards with the gate landing half on top of him.

"I've done it," he coughed.

Chaucer squeezed in beside him and helped him shove the gate to one side. "And now for our grand exit."

"Wait," Gregory lurched back into the cellar, forcing his way to the barred door at the other end. The smell of burning grew stronger and a muted crash came from overhead.

"Are you mad?" Chaucer cried. "We must go! Now!"

"The rebels... Their wine cellar isn't directly under the palace..." He broke off hacking and coughing in the sizzling air. But the men who'd locked them in the cellar could still be unaware of their danger. The smoke and heat wouldn't reach them until it was too late. Gregory would happily kill any of them in an honest fight. But leaving drunks to burn to death went against the grain.

He pounded his fists on the door, shouting hoarsely for them to run even as Chaucer tried to pull him away. For a moment, he thought he heard a voice raised in reply followed by more drunken laughter.

"Gregory," Chaucer's quiet tone broke through where his fear and fury had not, "it's no good. They are too drunk to heed you."

Gregory stared at him a moment, then nodded. They lurched back the way they'd come, squeezing past the gate and into the tunnel. Gregory had to walk half bent over but the tunnel grew cooler and cooler, and then river scented, summer air hit him in the face as they emerged at a small dock. A rowing boat was moored there and they clambered in, casting off from the dock. Gregory felt his senses returning to him as he filled his lungs again and again, coughing and gasping.

He shut his ears to the sound of men's voices screaming in terror from the direction of the tunnel. Surely it was his fancy. Such sounds could not travel so far against the noise of the fire and the creaking, tearing groans of collapsing timbers. And if it was not his imagination, there was nothing anyone could do for those men now.

Gregory turned to Chaucer and saw the poet's pale skin was reddened and smudged. His hair was singed and he reeked of sweat and fire. His clothes were in ruins. Gregory looked no better.

"It would seem I owe you my life once more." Chaucer made

an abortive attempt at his usual dry tone.

"I wouldn't normally thank a man for striking me in the face, but considering the circumstances I'll forego duelling you over it," Gregory said, eyes still fixed on the inferno that had once been the richest palace on the Strand.

There was a moment's silence, then Chaucer laughed so hard, Gregory thought the poet was going to fall overboard and was obliged to catch hold of his ruined doublet to keep him in the boat. Eventually, Chaucer stopped and wiped his eyes.

"What now?" Gregory said.

"What now indeed." Chaucer fixed his gaze soberly on the blaze.

There were rebels making regular trips down to the banks of the river and Gregory realised that they were carrying loads of valuables. At first, he thought they were looting. Having seen the riches in the meanest part of the palace – jewels and tapestries and fine cloth – Gregory almost didn't blame them. How much easier would his own life have been over the last few weeks if only he'd had the barest remnant of the Duke's fortune? And then he saw that the rebels were casting armloads into the Thames. Gold candlesticks and silver ewers. Chests containing who knew what wealth in coin and gems. They were burning the cloth of gold and the fine hangings.

"Are they mad?" Gregory realised he had spoken aloud.

"They're burning books!" Chaucer's tone was agonised. "Records and papers. Contracts and grants. But the books! The scrolls! History and poetry and philosophy!"

"It's just words," Gregory said, far more concerned with the depressing sight of a bag of gold coins splitting as one rebel flung it out over the water, its contents falling in gleaming homage to such fish as could be found here.

"Just words?" Chaucer said incredulously. "*Just words*? Maudesley, this happened due to words. Mere words – spoken, whispered, written – can change the world." He waved a grimy hand towards the river bank. "John Ball's words set them on this path when there was no other recourse for them."

"The cleric?" Gregory said.

"A man of God who did not bid them stay in their place and

serve their lords, but told them God intended for us all to be equal under Him." Chaucer shook his head. "What matter if those words were true? They set a fire in the hearts and minds of those who were dry kindling for them. You are a man of the sword. You know where wars are won, even before a drop of blood is spilt." The poet let out a breath. "And Balle was the least of it."

Gregory said nothing, seeing the vast shape his own dismissive utterance had failed to encompass.

Chaucer turned his face away from the destruction. "Words can topple a kingdom."

Gregory pondered that as the river carried them downstream.

13.

The baron did eventually arrive with the remainder of the dowry. Gregory returned home to find his wife entertaining her uncle in the hall. It had been nearly a week since Alienor had stormed out of the study. Gregory wasn't sure which of them was being more careful to avoid the other.

He watched as his wife rose gracefully and excused herself. "Surely you have matters to discuss which can have nothing to do with me," she said icily.

Gregory suppressed a grimace. He'd managed to hold on to his fury with her for almost an entire day. There were lords who would have dragged their wives back in such situations, by their hair if necessary. He'd never thought much of such men. It was unworthy to pit yourself physically against someone so much weaker than you, save for necessity in battle. Until that moment he had never before understood the temptation some men had dominate a woman with their fists. The idea was abhorrent to him. He would never countenance such behaviour in himself – another thing William had unwittingly taught him.

But Alienor *was* maddening.

"Is all well, Maudesley?" the baron enquired.

"Well enough, my lord." Gregory dragged his attention back to his guest.

The baron sipped from his goblet. "Such a show of maidenly modesty usually means my niece has schemes in hand. But perhaps you have broken her to bridle. There are inducements a husband may offer which an uncle may not, eh?"

"You'll not speak so of my wife, my lord," Gregory bristled before get a grip on his temper. The baron had been joking – rather tastelessly, it was true. Gregory couldn't fathom why he

96

was offended when mere moments before he'd been annoyed with Alienor himself.

The baron frowned at his tone but wisely shifted topics. He'd come with the remainder of the dowry, as well as to see how Alienor fared. Gregory bit back irritation over his wife's uncle checking her new husband was treating her well. The baron was clearly fond of his niece, despite his ribald jests. And the money was welcome even if the baron was not. Gregory waited out the visit with more patience than he knew he had.

Later, Gregory went up on to the curtain wall and looked out over his lands. Maudesley lands. Or they soon officially would be. He would ride for London tomorrow. It was too late in the afternoon to set out now. The air was sweet and mild, scented with the flowers blooming in the garden below. For the first time, it felt possible this truly would be his inheritance. It didn't seem the home of his boyhood now, nor was it haunted by William's memory. It was a new place. Somewhere he could settle. No more need to sell his sword to the highest bidder. A home. A wife. Perhaps sons? Gregory's mood soured. Not unless he mended matters with Alienor, something he had no idea how to accomplish.

Once he'd calmed down, he'd slowly and carefully read Alienor's summary of accounts and how they might be remedied. It was easier when he wasn't angry, when no one was watching how slowly he read. How he struggled. There had seemed to be much sense in his wife's suggestions, so he'd secretly shown the paper to his steward. Fletcher had endorsed Alienor's suggestions whole heartedly. Gregory had instructed Fletcher to proceed with whatever could be managed while the year was still good. But he had not told Alienor. To do so would be tantamount to an apology and he could not bring himself to do that. Let her find out when he was miles away in London and make of it what she would.

The sound of raised voices broke in on his thoughts. Gregory realised his wife was further down the wall, in conversation with a man who was not part of the castle household. He drew back into the long shadow cast by the nearest bastion. The stranger was walking very close to Alienor, speaking directly into her face as they drew nearer. Whatever he was saying had completely absorbed her attention. So much so that neither of them realised they were not alone on this stretch of the wall. Something hot and sour curdled in Gregory's gut. His nails dug into his palms. A second, longer look extinguished the sensation. Alienor looked almost as angry as she had when she'd stormed out of the study. Whoever the stranger was, he was no lover come to pay court. No doubt Alienor had been walking alone on the curtain wall, as was her habit, when the stranger had accosted her. And the sheer cheek of the interloper, prancing into Gregory's castle and seeking out his wife in her moment of solitude, without even tipping his cap to the baronet.

Gregory waited as they moved closer. He could be exceptionally quiet and still, for a big man. The breeze blew their voices to him and he caught the drift of the conversation.

"Do you know the punishment for adultery, my lady?" the stranger said, his voice an oily mixture of obsequiousness and disgust.

"I know it well." Alienor's March accent thickened in distress. "But it doesn't signify since I'm no adulteress. I've done nothing wrong."

"That is not the tale I hear," the stranger said, his fingers unconsciously stroking the nap of his finely made doublet. "It's the talk of the county that a certain lady got with child by a man who abandoned her, so she married an unlikely suitor to give her child a name."

"If that were true, then it would be my husband's business. If he raised no objections, it's nothing to you."

"My child, I am God's servant," the stranger said.

Gregory narrowed his eyes at the sight of the man's mushroom pale hand tucking a loose strand of Alienor's dark hair back. She recoiled as if his breath was foul or his touch disgusted her.

"As God's representative, I can assure you that the Almighty is very much concerned with these matters." The stranger's attempt at a sympathetic smile was laughable. "You are a long way from the Marches, my lady. Not all are sympathetic to your kind here. I shudder to think what a whisper of…shall we say sorcery? What result that might yield."

"You have a fool's gift for spinning yarns without a fool's wit to go with it. No one would…" Uncertainty entered her tone.

"No one would believe such accusations? Adultery and witchcraft?" The stranger chuckled. "Why else would the new baronet marry a Scot with a stained reputation? These are uncertain times and once an idea is sowed, it's very hard to uproot it. But it need not fall out in such a way. All you need do, is come to a hearing and prove your innocence. Accept your penance. Your new husband may even forgive your indiscretions."

Alienor's back was pressed against the battlements as she shrank from the stranger's touch. "You mean, I must pay a hefty sum to be officially pardoned and avoid punishment. I don't care what you think you know. I'm innocent and I won't line your pockets."

"Adultery carries a serious penalty."

"Adultery involves the breaking of wedding vows," Alienor snapped. "And I have not."

"Will your husband believe that, considering your history? Grim, suspicious man, I understand. Will he believe your protestations of innocence or will he believe as the rest of the county does?" The stranger smiled nastily. "Come, a little humility, a little money, and you can avoid unpleasantness. No one shall then tell your husband that your past misbehaviour was only the start."

Gregory had heard quite enough. He saw Alienor's eyes widen as he appeared behind the stranger, her lips parting in a soundless gasp, but all his attention was fixed on the greasy man in the fine doublet. Gregory seized him by the collar and belt, lifting him bodily so that his toes skated uselessly over the stone.

The stranger shrieked, kicking and struggling in futile panic. Gregory was in an ecstasy of rage too intense to be denied. This wretched, creeping scrap of offal had felt he could stroll in and extort money from the lady of the house. The lack of respect to Gregory's station would have infuriated him, if he'd thought about it. Then, all he could think of was how white Alienor's face had gone when the stranger disparaged 'her kind' and uttered the word 'witchcraft'.

"My lord...she is a harlot... she has been summoned..."

"My wife said she was innocent," Gregory roared. "If it's good enough for me, it's good enough for you. And for God too!"

He heaved squealing, struggling man into the air and threw him off the wall.

At the last moment, Gregory chose the bailey side of the curtain wall instead of the landward side. There was a scream and a muted, wet thud. In the sudden silence that followed, Gregory and Alienor exchanged a glance and peered over the edge. Below was the cart used to take night soil and other fragrant castle leavings to the midden.

Alienor pushed her hair out of her face and gave Gregory a complicated look. When she spoke, her voice was perfectly level. "Did you recall the honey cart was there, my lord?"

"Yes," Gregory said tersely.

"Was that before or after you threw him from the wall?" Alienor didn't look upset by his shocking loss of control. She looked as if she was trying very hard not to laugh.

"After," Gregory said, still full of pent up fury at the interloper. "I bloody hate summoners."

Alienor watched a group of castle folk gather around the honey cart, pointing and laughing at the summoner as he struggled to free himself from a sizeable pile of shit. "So I see."

"Yes. Well, if that's all, my lady," Gregory turned away but Alienor's small, white hand on his arm stopped him.

"You said my word was good enough for you," Alienor said.

He said nothing, already regarding his own actions with a touch of embarrassment.

"Gregory?"

He'd never heard her say his name before. Her accent changed it, clipping it into two lilting syllables. A different person. *Grey-Gree.* She watched him expectantly, scorn entirely absent. For the first time, he didn't feel he was being measured and found wanting.

"If you say you are not with child, I believe you," Gregory

admitted at last.

Alienor nodded. "And the rest?"

"It shouldn't matter," Gregory murmured. "You did not deceive me and I married you anyway."

"Yet it troubles you far more now, than it did when you came to court me," Alienor said. "Why is that?"

She was far too damned astute for his liking.

"I leave for London tomorrow," Gregory said, then went on deliberately, "your uncle brought the remainder of the dowry he owed me." Let her remember this was a transaction. It was her money he wanted. Only her money.

Alienor gave a brittle laugh. "I'll bid you a good journey then, my lord." She turned and swept back along the curtain wall, leaving Gregory to wonder what demon had possessed him, that he should end the first bit of civility between them with such an utterance.

14.

13th June, 1381

Gregory realised that they'd only reach Chaucer's home in Aldgate because the vast bulk of the Essex rebel horde had already passed through on the way to the Strand. By sheer luck they chose a time of comparative quiet, while the nearest groups of rebels had other things to occupy them. Those who went abroad today, did so at their peril. Or perhaps not. Gregory was inclined to agree with Chaucer's assertion that the rebellion had much support within the city, and that many Londoners had swelled its ranks. It seemed that the defences on London Bridge had been opened from the inside. Nothing had stood between the Kentish rebels and their destination as they crossed from Southwark.

Their second piece of luck was to find that Cuthbert had done as Gregory had ordered. Showing a pleasing flash of initiative, he had taken Drum and Patience, and the full saddlebags, and gone straight to Chaucer's home, rather than lingering on the streets. Gregory, who had been growing anxious about the boy's whereabouts – not to mention the whereabouts of his horse and money – was hit with a dizzying wave of relief when he discovered Cuthbert already waiting for him in the enclosed yard of Chaucer's residence. The boy was streaked with soot and dirt, and cracking streaks of dried blood from cuts and scratches, but otherwise unharmed.

"I thought you was burned," Cuthbert warbled, while tears made lighter tracks on his filthy cheeks.

"He's had a fright," Chaucer said wearily. "Don't be too hard on the lad. There's not many servants who would be so faithful as to wait with a prize warhorse in the face of riot and flames."

Gregory thought of the money in the saddle bags and flushed under the dirt and stink from the burning palace. He'd trusted

Cuthbert without thinking twice, and the boy had proved loyal and resourceful.

"It was well thought of to wait here," Gregory said.

"I remembered Master Chaucer said he lived in Aldgate," Cuthbert replied.

"Well done, lad. You were worth that shilling."

It was mean praise but Cuthbert swelled under it like a mating pigeon. "I saw this one man. He was trying to take away this big silver pot. But the other rebels caught him." The boy shivered. "You know what them rebels done to him? They grabbed him and threw him into the fire and the silver pot too. Said they weren't thieves and looters."

Chaucer and Gregory exchanged a look.

"We'll bathe and have dinner, then work out our next move. No doubt a messenger will come for me sooner or later," Chaucer said.

"Bathe?!" Cuthbert cried in horror. "I'm not bathing. It's not healthy."

Chaucer raised an eyebrow. "You'll bathe if you want to set foot in my house, and there's an end to it."

***

Peace did not descend with darkness. All across London, fires blazed in the black. The city burned and no act of destruction cooled the rebel rage. The Savoy Palace was not the only residence destroyed that day. The Marshalsea Prison in Southwark was torn apart; Clerkenwell Priory, home of the Knights Hospitaller, was destroyed, as was the nearby manor. The legal buildings and offices of the Temple on Fleet Street were a target of particular rebel wrath – they were ransacked and the records burned in the street, the tiles raked from the roofs to expose the buildings to the elements. The homes of law and court officials were burned, and when the rebels caught their owners, they executed them. The prison at Fleet and the one at Newgate were attacked, and the prisoners released.

Gregory had heard that many honest men and women were

imprisoned there for 'loitering' or 'wandering suspiciously' – an easy accusation to make when half the lords believed the Great Rumour. Such luckless individuals were detained as foreign spies, a clearly preposterous accusation. Others had been guilty of nothing more than being homeless, without work or too poor to purchase a pardon.

Gregory would happily throw all summoners and pardoners off the walls of Maudesley Castle given half an opportunity; he was not insensible to the injustice of the system. All the same, he thought the rebels would have done better to let the prisons alone because rapists, murderers, thieves and brigands had also doubtless been released. It was telling that the violence of the attacks increased greatly after the rebels took the prisons. The innocent died with the guilty, and corpses were stacked in the streets.

Rumours flew. Some was exaggeration spawned by panic. But there were intelligences that Gregory had to give credence to. He noticed how messages seemed to find their way into Chaucer's hands, even in the midst of the upheaval. The king's man indeed. Gregory would not make the mistake of thinking him merely a well-connected poet and clerk again.

"The king intends to ride out to meet the rebels," Chaucer said, early the following morning. "I think you should join his retinue."

Gregory looked up from his bread and beer. "The *king's* retinue? Why would I be welcome? I'm not known to him. I've never been at court."

"Most of the armies are in the north guarding against a Scottish incursion, under the Duke of Lancaster," Chaucer said. "They cannot be too picky about able swords."

"The king wants to ride out and confront the seething horde?" Gregory said. "The lad must have bigger balls than a man twice his age."

"The people claim they are loyal to the king," Chaucer pointed out.

Gregory grunted. "That didn't induce his majesty to disembark at Greenwich a few days ago, did it? Sensible of him."

"I believe the king's council prevented him from addressing the rebels," Chaucer said with a touch of reproach.

"So he plans to make another attempt to speak to them," Gregory said. "And just where is this happy occasion to take place?"

"Escaping from a burning building has put you in a wonderful mood," Chaucer said.

"That and being kept awake half the night by rebel merrymaking," Gregory said sourly. "I wouldn't be a Flemish weaver for all the gold in Christendom right now, would you?" Small bands of rebels currently roamed London, murdering any Flemings they found. The revolt was the perfect cover for settling old scores and jealousies.

"Such times bring out the worst in people," Chaucer said.

Gregory laughed harshly. "Such times bring out those who delight in violence and use the banner of a cause for their own ends. When lions hunt, the hyenas and jackals are never far behind."

"You speak as if you've seen such things before?" Chaucer said quietly.

"I dare say we'll all have seen such things before we're another day older." Gregory pushed his mug aside. "Tyler is keeping the rebels whipped into a frenzy, though God knows where he came from or what turned him into the spark that set the country alight."

"If what I have heard is true, he may not be acting entirely without cause," Chaucer said with a moué of distaste.

Gregory listened, stony faced, as Chaucer explained.

"It was the poll tax that did. That and how it was enforced. An unmarried woman is not liable to be taxed, whereas a married woman is," Chaucer said. "Allegedly, this led to families claiming a girl was unwed in order to avoid the tax."

"And how did those collecting the tax respond to that?" Gregory said grimly.

"They took the girls they suspected of being secretly married aside and inspected them." Seeing Gregory's scowl, Chaucer clarified. "The tax collectors in question attempted to discern whether the girls had lost their maidenheads, and could therefore be considered to be married, by er reaching up their skirts and… You can imagine the rest, Maudesley."

Gregory's hands tightened into fists. "I see. Is there anyone amongst the nobility who's still surprised the commons have risen against them? God's Blood."

"Parts of the system are corrupt, it's true," Chaucer said calmly.

"If someone had assaulted my daughter, I'd have something to bloody well say about it too," Gregory snapped. "And I'd be saying it with a sharp blade."

"That's as maybe, Maudesley, but you're a comparative rarity amongst the noble stock." Chaucer rubbed his eyes tiredly. "Some tales state that it wasn't Wat Tyler but another man – John Tyler or Tom Baker – who roused rebel sympathies when his daughter was assaulted. Whatever set Wat Tyler on this path, it would seem now that he is motivated far less by righteous fury and far more by personal gain. You cannot cure all the ills of a realm by tearing down one system without another to replace it. Tyler, from what I've heard, wants no system. He has taken Ball's sermons and gone a step further."

There was little Gregory could say to that. He knew the poet was right.

"Will you go as part of the retinue?" Chaucer said.

"Seems like that's the only way I'm going to meet the king," Gregory said. "Doesn't much serve my interests to let him die before he's accepted my oath."

15.

14th June, 1381

For all his flippant words, Gregory was dismayed to find himself making up part of a very small party protecting the king. The most experienced military commanders were all abroad in France, Germany or Ireland. With the army in the far north, only the Tower's garrison, the king's personal bodyguards and some two hundred or so soldiers remained. Chaucer had been correct. Knights were in far too short supply for Gregory's presence not to be welcomed as part of the retinue.

It was a strange enough company. Gregory was put in mind of that annoying, repetitive ballad about a young man calling for his friends on the way to a country fair – by the end of the song, the world and his wife accompanied the frivolous fool.

As well as the king's remaining military advisers – the Earls of Salisbury, Warwick and Oxford – the retinue contained Aubrey de Vere carrying the sword of state, Sir Thomas Percy, Sir Robert Knolles and William Walworth – the mayor of London. The king's mother, Joan, Princess of Wales, travelled just behind the king in a small carriage. The king's half-brothers – the Earl of Kent and John Holland – rode just a little ahead of Gregory, next to Jean of Gommegnies. Gregory thought Gommegnies must be shitting his braies about now, since it was well known that he'd been Gaunt's man for over a decade. The rebels wanted his head on a stick, to go with all the other heads on sticks they'd collected. Rounding out the party to a little under eighty warm bodies on horseback, rode assorted knights and squires.

Decidedly more squires than knights, Gregory noted grimly. The dearth of fully trained fighters was troubling, although considering the disparity in numbers, he wondered whether more knights would make much difference. There weren't enough warriors to engage the rebels if the volatile mass became violent. Certainly not enough to guarantee the safety of the king. Gregory felt horribly exposed every inch of the ride to Mile End.

The rebels clearly had allies inside the city. For all Gregory knew, they had bowmen stationed strategically at windows along the route the king would take. It wouldn't even need to be an assassination attempt on the king. There were hated notables of law and court here who would draw fire – Gommegnies being a case in point. Arrows missed their marks from time to time…and found other marks instead. Thanks to the king's grandfather, almost every peasant could use a longbow competently. The decree that every able bodied male over the age of nine should practise archery seemed like a double edged blade now. Gregory knew many women were also able archers, even if they tended to favour the short bow rather than the heavier, more difficult to draw six foot bows used in warfare. Short bows might be less powerful and have a shorter range, but that was scant comfort when an arrow from a short bow would dispatch you to the care of the Almighty just as handily as a longbow.

Gregory supposed the king's purpose in having so small an escort was to show the rebel leaders that he came with a number befitting his dignity and consequence, without being threatening. Bold but just what did this boy-king hope to accomplish? Could he not see that the rebels honoured the idea of him, rather than the fact? They might well agree to talk but Gregory did not believe that mere words would carry the day.

He stole a swift glance at the fourteen-year-old king, riding a fine grey mare ahead, surrounded by his immediate guard. The lad was tall for his age, and well formed in a way that promised athleticism when he reached his full height. Gregory supposed he was a relatively well favoured young man too, for all the good that would do him in the next few hours. He could at least applaud the decision to leave Simon Sudbury, the Archbishop of Canterbury, and Sir Robert Hales, the Lord High Treasurer, behind in the Tower. Though whether the king was concerned for their safety or wanting to distance himself from two unpopular ministers, it was hard to say.

"You look grim, friend," the knight riding on his left said.

Drum flicked his ears at the sound and Gregory tightened his hold on the reins minutely. "That's the way God fashioned my face."

The other knight chuckled. "Perhaps you could ride out in front and frighten the mob away then?"

"If I thought it would do any good, I'd be happy to oblige." Gregory regarded the other knight. He was a few years younger with reddish hair and a pleasant, open countenance. "How did you come to fall into such company?"

The other knight grinned. "What else are illegitimate younger sons good for?"

Gregory gave an amused snort. "Isn't that the truth."

"May I ask who I'm most likely going to die beside today?" The knight said, with a flash of gallows humour.

"Gregory Maudesley. And you, Sir…?"

"Bartholomew Ghent."

"Ghent? You're not related to the Duke of Lancaster, are you?"

"Would you hold that against me?" Ghent said. "No one can decide if I'm his bastard or not, including His Grace. I once thought that such a relation might be an asset but I'm just as glad not to be confirmed as His Grace's son today. The Duke did well to be on the Scottish border this week."

Gregory couldn't disagree with that, though having seen the hoarded wealth of the Savoy Palace, he privately thought the rebels might have a point about John of Gaunt. He was scrabbling to change the subject, when he noticed three riders peeling away from the middle of the procession. They disappeared into a side alley, followed by several other riders, squires and knights Gregory didn't recognise. He wondered if they'd been given separate instructions, then realised that the riders were the king's two half-brothers and Jean of Gommegnies. They were using the retinue as a means of escape.

"Let them go, Maudesley," Ghent said.

Gregory realised he'd been leaning forward in his saddle. "Is the king aware?"

"I'm sure His Majesty knows. It was inflammatory bringing those three. Perhaps this was the plan," Ghent said. "Clever really. Protection of numbers until they had a chance to hive off and get out of the city."

"I suppose they wouldn't make much difference if this goes ill," Gregory murmured. He didn't like it though. Rats deserting a sinking ship.

Mile End was a large, flat green area outside the city. A pleasant meadow for high days and holidays usually. Now it was a rebel encampment. There were lean-tos and make shift shelters, as well as signs of cooking fires. Subconsciously, Gregory ran a practised eye over the gathered rebels, estimating the numbers down to the last cudgel and bowstring. The verdict was an unpleasant one. There were thousands of rebels to less than a hundred knights and squires in the king's retinue. If the crowd became fractious, the outlook was poor for the king's party.

If Gregory had had any doubt that the rebels were well organised, the sight of the horde would have put paid to it. This was a focused and deadly army, well-armed with such weapons as could readily be made from farm and trade implements, not to mention the bows that were prominently carried by over half the crowd. It scarcely mattered that the common folk were not permitted to bear arms and therefore had no access to swords. A man or woman with a quarterstaff and the will to use it could do a lot of damage, even to a man in armour. And every blacksmith could fit a scythe blade to a five foot ash pole. This was no ill equipped rabble. The English army was made up chiefly of likely lads gleaned from the sons of villeins and common folk, set aside from day to day labour and trained in combat in small groups. They served as a pool from which a lord could draw his warriors, his men-at-arms and the troops he had to pledge to the king in times of war. The rebels had recognised the potential of utilising these trained men and recruited accordingly.

"I think Warwick's signalling you," Ghent said.

Gregory glanced down the line and saw that the Earl of Warwick was indeed waving him forward.

"It'll be that fearful glower," Ghent said. "Off you go. Put it to good use."

Gregory nudged Drum forward and the big horse huffed irritably.

"You there, Maudesley, is it?" Warwick said. "You're making up part of His Majesty's honour guard."

"Yes, my lord." Gregory knew damn well it wasn't a request. Judging from the other knights chosen, he guessed that it was his size and ferocious appearance that had got him selected for this particular honour. Nothing like being a big man on a big horse when there was a king to protect, in the face of excitable rebels with bows.

A small group of rebels stood slightly forward of the crowd. To Gregory's eyes they appeared confident but tense. There was no way of knowing how this talk would go. He sensed no immediate threat. He did not believe this to be a scheme to get the king out of the Tower and into bow range. There had already been ample opportunity for that. But there was a palpable tension to the air. Gregory would not be lowering his guard. At a signal from Warwick, Gregory joined the others in forming a guard around the king. He shifted uneasily.

Aubrey de Vere moved forward first, brandishing the sword of state before announcing His Majesty, King Richard. The small honour guard moved forward with the king at their centre. Gregory was on the outermost right corner, glaring at the crowd, so he did not see Richard ride forward, parting the guard in front of him, though from the silence that fell over the crowd, Gregory guessed that was what the king had done. It had the feel of ceremony to it. As if rustics, tradesmen and merchants demanding the king's presence were an occasion with historical precedence. Allowing them the sense that they were important to their monarch. Gregory admired the cleverness of this strategy even as he kept his attention on the rebels. Was that man in the brown cowl tightening his hand on a bowstring? Or was it Gregory's own hyper alertness that was making him think so? He breathed smoothly and shallowly, trying to allow everything to flood his senses without overwhelming them. The trick was not to fixate on a single detail in a situation that might

111

turn violent. That might well get you killed because other clues were missed.

"Good folk of England," Richard said. "Honest countryfolk and hardworking townspeople." The young king had the knack of pitching his voice so it would carry. There was no tremulous quality, no sense that Richard was nervous or aware that he was in danger. He paused and Gregory found he was hanging on the king's words as much as the rebels seemed to be. "I am come amongst you, my people, to hear your grievances. Tell me your trouble."

God in heaven, Gregory thought. *He makes it sound like it was his own idea, not a gambit to get the mob out of the city.*

"Who speaks for you?" Richard said.

The crowd murmured, as if unwilling to trust the king's words. Gregory kept his breathing even when it would have stilled in his throat. This was the tipping point. A wrong word, a breath might sway them one way or the other.

"This will not do," Richard said. "Squire!"

Gregory did not dare take his eyes from the crowd but a gasp from behind him and a flicker of movement in his peripheral vision, had him instinctively flanking the other honour guard as they moved forward. King Richard had dismounted. He would meet his people on foot, eye to eye. It was an extraordinary concession, and it was working. The mood of the crowd had lifted. Three figures stepped forward from the group – two men, one woman. They bowed to the king who nodded gravely in return. Gregory hastily dismounted with the other guards, keeping pace with the king.

"Which of you is Master Tyler?" Richard said, looking at the men.

"Neither of us, your majesty," one of the men said. "I'm Thomas Caulder. This is Johanna Ferrours and Jem Wilkins."

"I see," Richard said. A faint shadow of trouble passed over his young face. "Well then Master Caulder, we meet at a time of great discord. I would hear your troubles and see what may be done to assuage them. I would have all my people return to their homes, content in the knowledge that their woes have been heard and, where possible, alleviated. Will you tell me?"

He spoke to Caulder but his voice was pitched to carry to the crowd. Those at the front passed Richard's words back and the mob relaxed another degree. Gregory noticed that some put down their bows and staves. It was true. They considered themselves loyal subjects of the king. They did not wish to harm him.

Emboldened by Richard's cordial words, Caulder began to speak, occasionally Wilkins would put in a word. Johanna Ferrours was a stout, strong, hard featured woman of middle years. When she spoke her words were sharp but insightful. Gregory could see how she had claimed a place at the head of the horde.

And then he really listened to what they asked of the king and his mind reeled. They wanted no man or woman to be forced to serve another except by his own will. They wanted the freedom to sell their produce where they chose; that any market should be accessible to those who had goods to sell. They wanted land rents to be set at four pence per acre across the kingdom, save where such rents were already set lower. They deemed that none gathered here who had taken part in the revolt should be punished for his actions, but allowed to depart in peace back to his own lands.

Gregory saw the shape of a new England that the rebels had sketched out. It was a bold design, huge in scope. It would change the face of the nation. Chaucer had argued that the rebels were not a mob of disgruntled and violent rustics, but an organised force with a plan. Gregory had believed the poet and here was proof that their plan was sophisticated beyond even Master Chaucer's imaginings. The rebels wanted an end to villeinage – no more should a man be the property of another. They wanted an end to the money grabbing monopolies of the abbeys and priories and great houses, who said that their tenants must give them produce in tribute and obliged them to use their mills and pay high rates to do so.

Gregory had scarce begun to comprehend how this might affect him personally – although he had a dim sense of gratitude that Fletcher had already begun on Alienor's suggested improvements – when he realised that King Richard was saying yes.

Yes, no man should be the bondsman of another so long as he was loyal to his king.

Yes, those who grew their crops and tended their animals should have the power to decide when and where produce was sold, and not be forced to purchase services from their liege lords.

Yes, four pence per acre was a reasonable rent and should be set as such across the kingdom.

And if they would accept their king's word and seal, none who departed peacefully without further violence, should be sought for retribution.

It was staggering. Gregory thought that the young king was merely telling them what they wished to hear, then revised his opinion. Richard clearly agreed with the rebels on a number of points. He truly did not believe that villeinage was fair or ordained by God. He meant everything he was offering them, if only in that moment. And he grew in stature under the attention his people were showing him. It occurred to Gregory that perhaps the councils formed to help Richard rule, had indeed been stifling the king's voice. Did Richard see this as an opportunity to claim at least some of his autonomy as king?

And then Caulder said, "and we want the heads of the chief perpetrators on charges of treason against your majesty's people and thus against your majesty. They have lined their own pockets to the detriment of the kingdom and its people."

There were angry cries of approval from the crowd. Gregory tensed reflexively. The rebels still wanted blood. They were not all of one stripe with their demands. Some, no doubt, wanted to settle personal scores far more than they wanted everything else Richard had agreed to. And there was no way to weed malcontents and criminals out of the general mob.

"Who are these chief perpetrators who have so offended Our people and thus Ourself?" Richard said.

Caulder gave a list of names. It was modest in length but contained some of the most illustrious personages of the kingdom. The Duke of Lancaster. Simon Sudbury, Archbishop of Canterbury. Robert Hales, Lord High Treasurer. John Legge and John Bampton, who had attempted to collect unpaid poll taxes. Sir Ralph Ferres. Chief Justice Robert Bealknapp. And John Fordham, Keeper of the Privy Seal.

Richard listened to this with grave courtesy. Gregory had to give the lad credit for his self-possession. He didn't so much as twitch as the rebels demanded that the most powerful men in England, saving himself, should be handed over to the mob.

"Those who you have named belong to me for punishment, if retribution is needful." Richard said. "All those who are traitors and may be proved as such by due process of law shall be freely seized and punished."

There was a moment of silence after the king's words that stretched out taut as a snare's wire, then the crowd erupted into cheers.

Gregory felt a twinge of misgiving. Richard's carefully worded reply had not promised the rebels that they should be the ones to mete out justice, or indeed that their preferred flavour of justice would be dealt at all. And yet from the way the rebels reacted, Richard might as well have signed death warrants for those most hated of men.

A contingent of rebel leaders was elected to accompany the king and his immediate guard back to the king's townhouse – better known as The Wardrobe – where a team of monks would be put to work drawing up letters of manumission, and charters of all that Richard had promised. Gregory was surprised to find himself once more drafted into the king's guard but made no protest as he remounted Drum.

He thought again that today might well be the first time Richard had ever acted unilaterally as king. His advisors had not been present. And because Richard had the Privy Seal on his person – John Fordham having fled in terror – there was no need to go through the lengthy process of putting a proposal before his counsel and applying for use of the seal. Richard had flexed his royal prerogative and decided entirely as his own intellect and conscience moved him. Gregory was certain when the king's council discovered this day's work, they were going to be apoplectic with rage. He cast a glance at the king riding in front of him and oddly an image of Alienor came to his mind.

Perhaps they were both right and a master worth serving was one who did not own his servants, but commanded their loyalty with his own worthiness; who dealt with them fairly and did not set himself so high above them, that they ceased to be people. He could see the dim shape of an as yet unformed future and perhaps it would be a better one. England had changed since the war in France began, since the days of the Black Pestilence. Was still changing. Only the foolish and those too old or too invested in the way things had always been, would resist that truth. But Gregory knew that change was not so simple.

This rebellion was far from over.

***

The news reached the king's party at the Great Wardrobe later that day, and bore out all of Gregory's misgivings. The reason the famous Wat Tyler had not been present for the audience with the king was simple. He and another rebel leader, named Jack Straw, had broken into the tower with a splinter group of rebels. Although 'broken in' was too strong a term, since the gates had apparently been opened for them.

Cuthbert had been left in the charge of the head groom at the Tower stables when Gregory had joined the king's retinue. Gregory would not allow himself to dwell on the boy's fate, but he'd been the first to volunteer to join the party of knights and men-at-arms who would ride back and examine the damage at the Tower. The rebels had long departed by the time they arrived. Apparently, having done what they set out to do at the Tower, the rebels had moved back into London in search of other 'traitors' or, as Gregory more cynically supposed, Flemings – who would be executed merely for being foreign and wealthy.

No one yet knew whether the Tower gates had been opened through trickery, coercion or the actions of a sympathiser within the king's household staff. Either way, it had been a calculated strike against the rebels' hated enemies.

Simon Sudbury was dead. The rebels had dragged the Archbishop of Canterbury from the Tower, to the traditional place of execution on Tower Hill, and beheaded him. The Lord High Treasurer, Robert Hales, had met with the same fate, as had John Legge, the king's sergeant at arms, and the lawyer, Richard Somenour. Gregory gazed down at the headless corpses, which had been left where they had fallen. The body of a friar lay decapitated nearby on the red washed ground.

Bartholomew Ghent toed the body over onto its back. "Appleton." He glanced up at Gregory, all trace of his former good humour gone. "He was a physician and surgeon favoured by His Grace, the Duke of Lancaster. I doubt anyone will weep for Sudbury or Hales. You don't get that rich without offending your peers and crushing your inferiors. They were useful, not likeable."

Gregory nodded, wondering why Ghent would risk such borderline treasonous talk. And then it truly struck home. The rebels – ordinary men and women not raised to nobility as ordained by God – had dared to invade the king's residence and murder those under his protection. It cut the legs out from beneath accepted social order. Word would spread. Never again would a peasant or tradesman's obedience to his lord be unquestioning. Doubt about the rightness of social hierarchy would lodge like a thistle seed in even the most unfertile minds.

"They took the heads?" Gregory said, partially to interrupt his own thoughts.

"On pikes," Ghent confirmed. "I imagine said heads will be decorating the bridge by now."

"There's not much damage other than..." Gregory waved a hand at the abandoned corpses. "The rebels took nothing."

"No damage?" Ghent exclaimed. "One of the men-at-arms said it took eight blows of a rebel axe to take Sudbury's head. Maudesley, surely you can see what this means?"

"It means they should have used a sharper axe," Gregory grunted.

"The blood in your veins must be like icemelt." Ghent shook his head. "Do you fear nothing?"

"A great many things, none of which are of immediate

concern," Gregory said. "Was the king's cousin not also in residence?"

"Sweet Jesu! I had forgotten." Ghent cast an eye over the corpses again but there was obviously no teenaged boy amongst them. "Did he escape?"

"We have to be sure, one way or another."

Ghent nodded, then hurried towards the White Tower.

Gregory started for the stables, intent on discovering what had become of Cuthbert. If the boy had come to no harm, he thought he would box his ears for him.

The stable was dim and cool, smelling of clean hay and horse. One of the few horses left behind when the retinue rode out, poked its long muzzle over the stall door and snorted. Gregory spotted the ambler, Patience, resting a leg in another stall. The rebels had not set fire to anything at the Tower at least. He supposed the benefit of those who revolted being farmers and tradesmen was that they wouldn't wilfully destroy crops or produce, or harm livestock.

"Lad? Where are you?" Gregory called softly. "Cuthbert?"

There was a muffled thud and a small, skinny figure emerged from the gloom beside the empty loose box. "My lord?"

Gregory released a breath and the tight knot in his gut loosened. "You are without doubt the most expensive shilling I ever spent," he said crustily.

Cuthbert grinned. "We hid. When they came, I mean. There's big lofts up there." The boy pointed up. "They didn't do more than glance in here to see if anyone was hiding."

"And no one found you," Gregory said relieved. Not that the boy should have been in any danger but still. "What do you mean 'we'?"

"Me and the other lad. That man Ferrour brought him in here. Told us to get up the ladder sharpish. 'Cept now he won't come down."

Gregory went over to the long ladder leading up to the hay lofts. "Get Patience ready, Cuthbert. We'll not be staying." He ascended the ladder carefully, testing each rung. Peering over the lip into the hay loft, he called, "you can come out now, my lord."

For a moment there was silence, then a pile of hay at the far end stood up and moved into the light. The lad was slender and tall for his age, but there the resemblance to the king ended. Henry Bolingbroke was most definitely John of Gaunt's son, the hard, sharp, clever features already beginning to push through the childish roundness of his face.

"Have they truly gone?" Henry said.

"Yes, my lord," Gregory replied. "And most relieved His Majesty will be to see you unharmed."

Henry's eyes were wide and his face was very pale. "They were going to kill me," he said, voice flat with shock. "They wanted to murder me, because of my father."

Gregory nodded but Henry wasn't finished.

"I tried to hide in the Tower. I know it wasn't very brave but—"

"Living to fight another day is good sense. It's important to be clever as well as brave," Gregory said gruffly.

Henry made his way towards the ladder. "One of the rebels found me. John Ferrours. He made me put on a servant's tunic and then snuck me into the stables. Your servant piled hay on me and said if the rebels started searching the lofts, he would distract them."

"Did he?" Gregory had made his way down the ladder by this point and threw a sour look at Cuthbert. Of course the young fool had offered that. More courage than sense.

Henry stepped down onto the stable floor. He was shivering but held himself straight. "I am ready to go, when you think it meet."

Gregory's brows unknit slightly. The lad was very nearly as brave as his cousin. He'd known men twice this boy's age who'd succumbed to vapours in milder circumstances. "Do you have a horse, my lord?"

Henry pointed out a chestnut palfrey and Cuthbert hurried to saddle it.

"Let's meet up with the rest of the guard and be off then," Gregory said.

"May I have your name, sir...?" Henry said.

"Maudesley."

"Sir Maudesley. You have my gratitude, you and your servant. Cuthbert, is it? I will not forget your names," Henry said, and took the reins of his horse.

"He knows my name," Cuthbert whispered.

Gregory followed the Duke of Lancaster's son out of the stables, cuffing Cuthbert on the shoulder as he went. "Stop grinning, lad. He hasn't elevated you to the peerage."

16.

14th June, 1381

Aside from the half dozen beheadings, the violence at the Tower had been confined to property. There had been the odd scuffle with a couple of men-at-arms. The Princess of Wales' lady of the bedchamber had been mocked and insulted into a fainting fit. The king's bed had been attacked and hacked at with swords – not an insult levelled at the king but at those he received there on state business.

Gregory tried to imagine receiving his wealthier tenants in his own bed chamber while he sat up in the huge featherbed Alienor had so recently banished him from, and decided that traditional or not, he would far rather face a man with a grievance on his feet. Or at the very least, seated in a hall.

The rebels had left everyone else unscathed. Yet, as Gregory had realised on Tower Hill, it could scarcely be worse. The message was clear – either the king could not or would not protect those the rebels deemed traitors. The government was in a shambolic state. The chancellor and the treasurer were both dead, and those suitable to hold the office were now all too terrified to be prevailed upon to accept the roles. The machinery for running the kingdom had ground to a halt. Meanwhile, pockets of violence and theft in the city continued to grow, as those rebels who remained bullied and extorted money and food from Londoners in order to feed themselves. There was no clear law and order. No way of bringing thieves and murderers to swift justice. The situation was critical.

Richard, having temporarily entrusted the Great Seal to the Duke of Arundel, called a session of the council. All the available clerks were still at work on letters of manumission, which Richard clearly thought prudent to allow to continue for now. So Chaucer, the only available clerk not employed in such a manner, was drafted to make notes. Gregory was surprised to find himself also called upon to attend.

Sir Walter Grey, the marshal of the king's guard, had cast a shrewd, steely gaze over those who'd recently come from the Tower and had inexplicably chosen Gregory to give an account of what had been found. He did so as succinctly as possible, then took a position near the door of the chamber, as the council debated.

"They have made me look a fool," Richard said. He had a soft, stammering mode of speech when he was uncertain.

It was true. The rebel splinter group had gambled on Richard bringing most of his men with him to Mile End, and leaving behind those whose presence would especially offend the mob. To an outside observer, it looked as if Richard had abandoned Sudbury and Hales to their fate, especially considering the ease with which Tyler and company had entered the Tower. There would be more than a few folk who would wonder if Richard had not deliberately left the drawbridge down, so to speak. And all the while, Richard himself was granting their demands.

"Those letters of manumission cannot be allowed to stand," the Earl of Salisbury said heatedly. He and the rest of the council had been repeating themselves on the matter with great politeness but increasing emphasis for the last hour. "We were not consulted on such an action, nor would we have agreed to it if we had been. Your Majesty was in a difficult position, of course, but with respect–"

"I have heard all your complaints, Salisbury," Richard said in an icy tone. In that moment he was every inch a king and not a stripling youth of fourteen.

Whatever might have been the wiser course of action, kings did not apologise nor explain their actions. Salisbury was in danger of forgetting himself. Richard's fair skin was flushed with barely contained anger. A man's anger, not a boy's. Gregory thought that Richard was offended by his council's attitude as concerned his royal prerogative, and mortally insulted and enraged at the duplicitous actions of the rebels. Here were two groups of England's people, both wielding their own version of power, and the result was to pat the king on the head as 'knowing no better for he was but a lad'.

"What do you think?" Richard said, turning a snapping gaze on Gregory with startling suddenness.

"Me, Your Majesty?" Gregory said in surprise.

"Yes, you. I do not know you, do I? And yet you marched fearlessly enough forward as part of my guard at Mile End, then volunteered to enter the Tower after the rebel attack, bringing Our cousin back to Us." The king paused, considering. "You have not known and advised me since I was a child. You can have no more love for me than as your king. So I will hear your counsel."

Gregory wondered if the king intended to insult his advisers, several of whom looked highly affronted that a mere country knight of no great fame should be called upon to speak. "Your Majesty," Gregory began, well aware that even if the king could afford to offend his notables, Gregory could not. "I am but a simple soldier at heart. I would hesitate to advise Your Majesty in such circumstances."

"My son asked for your opinion, Sir Maudesley. That is your name, is it not?" Joan, the Princess of Wales, had the same sharp, dark eyes as her son. She had been lauded as a great beauty in her youth and outlived three husbands. In her fifth decade she was formidable.

"Yes, Your Highness," Gregory made a short bow, wondering how the king's mother knew him when no one else did.

"I thought so," the Princess of Wales said. "You have a look of your mother. Well? Are you going to answer your king?"

"Your Highness—"

"Yes, yes, you weren't schooled to eloquence and rhetoric. Very good, you shall not lie as smoothly as others do," she said tartly. "Here are a dozen clever men to advise my son and not one of them can look at the matter at hand." Joan cast a disparaging glance over the council. "They're a lot of bilious old sheep and I tire of their bleating."

"Mother," Richard said firmly, a touch of reproof in his tone.

"Oh very well. Shall we hear Maudesley or not? What say you, sir knight?"

Gregory caught sight of Chaucer turning away. He thought

the poet was smoothing away a smile with his fingertips, though to another observer it might look like he was merely stroking his beard in thought. Gregory swallowed, aware that he was sweating as if he had been required to read a document in front of an onlooker. To his relief his voice came out strongly.

"My opinion, Your Majesty, is that in every gathering of such as we saw at Mile End, there will be those who devoutly believe in the cause they follow. Those people might be appealed to by reason, just as Your Majesty did so." Gregory was aware of the unblinking gazes of the council. He had everyone's attention now. Sod them, the lords so intent on protecting their monopolies, their right to own villeins that they could not see past it well enough to understand what a blow had been dealt to English governance. He no longer cared if he offended them or not. The king's mother was right. "But there are always wolves dressed as sheep. Some of them believe the agenda of the flock will never be carried far enough. And some are there because they scent blood. It's all one to them who wins or loses, they just want to be at the kill."

"Go on." Richard might have started this as a way to annoy his council but now he was listening. "What would you do?"

"There's not much use trying to get a pack off your trail when you've cut chunks off the slaughtered stag and fed it to them. A taste of flesh will have the wolves snapping at your heels forevermore." At the last moment Gregory stopped himself following the metaphor to its logical conclusion. He met the king's gaze and saw that Richard had followed it without help. What was more, he was certain the king agreed with him. Having agreed to rebel demands in good faith, Richard had encouraged the wolves.

"And what would you do, Sir Maudesley?" Richard said, voice deadly soft.

It occurred to Gregory that there was a fearsome intellect behind the fourteen-year-old king's eyes. For a moment he wondered if Richard's plan to distract his advisors from their grievances by deflecting their attention on to Gregory had worked even better than the young king had hoped, and now the lad was capitalising on it.

"Many of the rebels left after the audience yesterday. Almost all those from Essex and a good number from Kent. They were content with your Majesty's word. We are still outnumbered but less so."

"It matters little if we are outnumbered a hundred to one or ten to one," Warwick snapped. "It will still be the death of us in open confrontation."

"I'm aware of that, my lord," Gregory said. "But those left are the hard core contingent of rebels. They'll make further demands now they're feeling confident, having tasted blood."

"What sort of demands could they possibly make now?" the Earl of Salisbury said. "They already wish to overturn the entire country with their notions of free labour and free market!"

"Surely you have more imagination than that, Salisbury," the Princess of Wales said silkily. "I can think of half a dozen demands. The right to appoint the next Archbishop of Canterbury for example. That cleric...what was his name? Ah yes, John Ball. How should you like that radical excommunicate in charge of Mother Church in England?"

"You clearly see an opportunity here, Sir Maudesley," Richard said. "Let us hear it."

"They will be open to another audience," Gregory said. "Perhaps you might persuade them to depart as you did with so many at Mile End. But if not, it would be an excellent occasion to take the head wolf and disperse the pack that way."

"Are you out of your wits?" Robert de Vere, the Earl of Oxford said. He was a scant handful of years older than Richard. Young for an earl and a military advisor. "The danger to his majesty would be extreme."

"It is a strategy with much risk, it's true," Gregory said. "There would need to be a militia standing by in the city to help put down any resistance. His Majesty would need the finest knights as his personal guard."

"Pick a fight with Tyler," Warwick said slowly.

"Are you endorsing this madness?" Salisbury demanded.

"Maudesley is correct save for one aspect. It will not be enough to remove Tyler. He must be discredited," Warwick said.

"Out of the question," Robert de Vere said.

"What is *your* plan, my lord?" Richard said.

De Vere said nothing.

"Anyone?" Richard looked at the gathered notables. No one had anything to add. The King turned to Gregory again. "How great is the danger?"

"If it means adding what my lord of Warwick is suggesting, the danger is significant, Your Majesty," Gregory said. "Nine hundred long bows were stolen from the armoury when the rebels invaded the tower. It only takes one to kill a man in the hands of a moderately skilled archer."

"But it can be done?" Richard said.

Reluctantly, Gregory nodded then remembered he was required to answer more fully. "I believe so, Your Majesty. But it's a great risk. If your advisers can think of any other way, I would as leif do that."

Richard regarded Gregory for a moment, dark eyes weighing him against some unknown internal measure. He gave a slight nod. "They will not aim at their king and it is best to check them now and check them hard, before they reach a point where they are willing to do so. Or before they burn more of London. We will do as you advise."

He looked to Warwick and told him to make what arrangements he saw fit to ensure success and safety. "But I want Tyler taken alive. He must be tried and discredited through process of law. The rebels believe, at present, that God is on their side. They must discover that He is not."

Gregory didn't point out that in his experience God had little to say in such matters.

17.

15th June, 1381

Early the following morning, King Richard and his retinue – those who had accompanied him to Mile End and as many of the garrison and additional soldiers as could be spared – rode down the Strand towards Westminster. Gregory had been advanced up the train and now held a place directly behind the king. He wasn't sure whether it was Warwick's doing or Richard's, but he recognised the honour, even as a hard, cynical part of his mind reminded him of the added risk. Wynnstree and Gregory's struggles to take possession of it seemed miles away and decades ago.

Those who had not yet seen the devastation wreaked on London by the rebels gasped or swore softly into the hush that lay over the train. Drum snorted and tossed his head when he scented smoke, and Gregory murmured to the big horse soothingly. The ruins of what had once been the richest palace in England, still smouldered.

The king called a halt at Westminster Cathedral, where he and his immediate guard dismounted and entered. Even as Gregory stood respectfully back, waiting as Richard knelt to pray at the tomb of his ancestor, Edward the Confessor, his long held cynicism spiked him. No doubt Richard was sincere in his prayers but the image of a promising and pious young king would do him no harm, would it? And they might have taken another route to meet with Tyler and the remaining rebels. Gregory thought Richard had deliberately chosen the Strand and Westminster Cathedral so that his entire retinue would see what was at stake. He wanted them to remember that they served themselves when they served their king.

Having sought the blessing of his sainted forebear, Richard led his train on to the vast green meadow outside the city.

Smithfield was where the weekly livestock markets were usually held. At one end stood the Priory of St Bartholomew and the hospital of the same name. The rebels were waiting for them.

If the mood at Mile End had been wary and tense, it had also been cautiously hopeful. Gregory thought that those who had treated with the king that day had done so in good faith. Perhaps they had not even known what mischief was being done at the Tower as they made their requests. The mood today was different. Tense certainly, as was to be expected when one armed party met another. But there was none of that honest hopefulness beneath the alert gazes of the crowd. There was something else, Gregory decided. An insolent acquisitiveness that promised a far uglier turn to the proceedings. He didn't like the feel of this.

A small contingent of rebels were mounted on horseback. Amblers rather than fine destriers or coursers; Richard's party had the better mounts. Still, it was telling that they should decide to meet the king they claimed to honour and love, not on foot as betokened the appropriate level of humility to their liege, but on horseback as if they were combatants facing each other down the lists.

"Maudesley?" The king said in a low voice.

"Yes, sire?"

"Stay by my side." The corner of Richard's mouth tensed as if he was attempting to prevent another expression spreading on his face.

Gregory mentally applauded his courage. Only someone who had been scared just as green themselves, would recognise that supreme effort to master fear. "Of course, sire."

It would only occur to him later how strange it was that the king should look to him first for support, and that just as naturally he had offered it.

A small, pre-chosen group of the king's train rode forward with Richard at their heart. Gregory rode on the king's right, and to his right rode Sir John Newenton. Gregory knew many of the others by sight now. John Philipot. Nicholas Brembre. Robert Launde and the aging Ralph Standissh. The Earl of

Salisbury brought up the rear. Sir Bartholomew Ghent rode behind the king and to the left, a sardonic smile on his face. Gregory counted another eight knights and half a dozen esquires. The rest of the train hung back under Warwick's command.

The king lifted a hand and Salisbury called a halt some distance from both the rebels and the remainder of the train.

"Sir Newenton? Ride over and bid Master Tyler approach," Richard said.

"Y-yes, sire." Newenton cleared his throat nervously then kicked his mount forward.

Gregory watched as he approached Tyler's party. One of the mounted rebels edged forward on his grey ambler. A large, stout man in a leather jerkin. Even from here, it was easy to see that his face was reddened either by working outdoors or excessive ale, or both.

Newenton and Tyler halted their horses. Tyler said something, to which Newenton replied but Gregory could not tell what was said at such a distance. They appeared to be arguing. Even now Tyler did not dismount – a clear piece of insolence. Gregory thought that Newenton tensed. He recalled suddenly, that Newenton had lost Rochester Castle after a nominal defence during one of the first attacks of the revolt. He sincerely hoped Newenton had not been sent to bring Tyler forward as punishment. The situation was too precarious for such conceits. At length, however, Tyler waved a hand to his fellow mounted rebels and they rode towards the waiting party of the king. Wat Tyler on his grey horse rode a little ahead with Newenton.

"Now you will dismount," Gregory heard Newenton say furiously. "In the presence of your king, you will approach on foot."

Tyler did not dismount. Nor did he doff his cap. He looked Richard over with a casual appraisal that no man should employ in presence of his betters. Perhaps it was bravado. Tyler was, after all, merely a roofer who'd found an opportunity to lead, yet here he was surrounded by men of standing who were educated far and beyond him. No amount of native wit and natural cleverness could ameliorate the sense of insignificance that must occasion. Gregory understood that better than he wished. Then Tyler grinned and Gregory realised the man was drunk on his success. To all intents and purposes, he'd enjoyed the privileges of a lord for the last few days.

"Master Tyler," Richard said courteously.

"Your Majesty, be of good comfort and joyful, for within the fortnight you shall have forty thousand more of the commons than you have now, and we shall be good companions." Tyler delivered this extraordinary speech in a gleeful, rambunctious tone.

Gregory knew he wasn't the only person to find Tyler's words both elliptical and disturbing. He cut his eyes sideways and saw that Richard's expression did not flicker.

"Well, Master Tyler, I am come to hear why my subjects are still gathered *en masse* in London instead of returning to their homes as was agreed not two days since," Richard said.

Tyler's expression of unimpressed arrogance darkened. "I wasn't at Mile End. Those who spoke didn't present all the demands."

Richard's eyebrows rose a little at the word 'demands' but he kept his tone level. "Let us hear these further *requests*."

Gregory listened with mounting disgust as Tyler laid out what further concessions the rebels wanted. Was this bumptious, arrogant, loud fool the head wolf? And yet Gregory knew he had been correct – those rebels remaining were those who had little interest in returning home. They wanted more. They had enjoyed their power and were in no hurry to settle back into their lives.

A restive murmured travelled through the king's guard on hearing Tyler's demands. No law but the law of Winchester. All preserves of water, parks and woods to be made free to all, so all throughout the kingdom, wealthy and poor should be at liberty to take game and fish, and hunt the hares in the fields. A removal of Church hierarchy save for a single prelate over all of England – the king's mother had been right, Gregory was almost amused to note. All property belonging to religious communities and clergy – save enough for reasonable subsistence – to be removed from its current owners and divided amongst the commons. A stop to fees for burials and Christenings.

Richard listened to Tyler's increasingly emphatic and excited demands with a smooth expression. Finally Tyler trailed off and Richard replied.

"I will grant all I reasonably can, saving the regality of the crown. And now, Master Tyler, you will go to your followers and commend them to return to their homes."

"That's not good enough," Tyler blurted, stung by the king's circumspect tone. "Our letters patent need to be amended before a single man amongst us will go anywhere."

"Master Tyler, you try my patience," Richard said. "Twice I have come and listened to my people. I have made a great many concessions already. And when I have had time to convene my council to discuss your requests, I may yet grant more. On the understanding that all of those still encamped here leave this very day."

"And you try *my* patience!" Tyler cried. "Years we have laboured, working our fingers raw, only for some fat lord or bishop to steal the fruits of our labours while our own children go hungry. It isn't right in the sight of God and it shouldn't be right under law. The good Lord never meant for us slave for luxuriant thieves!"

In the moment of shocked silence that followed, a man laughed loudly. Gregory realised it was Ghent, his carefree voice loud enough for all to hear.

"Thieves? Oh that's a good joke Master Tyler. I hear you stole a chest containing one thousand marks not two days ago. And now you're back demanding more? Why you're the biggest thief of all." Ghent grinned viciously. "A thief and a traitor!"

Tyler's red face went cheese pale with fury. "How dare you!" He pulled a dagger from his waist and brandished it at Ghent, and in so doing, waved a naked blade at the king.

"He threatens the king!" Newenton bellowed, sawing on his mount's reins to put himself between Tyler and Richard.

Tyler, panicking at a fully armoured knight on horseback bearing down on him, stabbed his dagger at Newenton. It

131

glanced harmlessly off the knight's breastplate but murder had been attempted.

Gregory was trying to edge Richard's horse away from the conflict by inserting himself and Drum in the way, so he saw Newenton choose not to draw his sword but take up his own dagger instead. Even then, he thought Newenton meant to crack Tyler across the back of the skull with the pommel to stun him, but something went wrong and a wide, scarlet cut opened across the back of Tyler's neck. The blow sent him tumbling from his horse and in his panic, as the other mounted rebels surged forward screaming their fury, he lashed about with his dagger, blindly cutting one horse and causing another to throw his rider.

Only Old Ralph Standissh kept his head, wheeling his horse and stabbing his sword between Tyler's chest and shoulder, so that his dagger wielding arm fell uselessly to the ground. The unmounted rebels surged forward and in response, here came all the king's men. Everything happened in short, bright flashes and somewhere, Gregory heard Ghent laughing like a madman, as the carefully drawn plan for capturing Tyler alive fell into ruins beneath the frenzied, thrashing hooves of warhorses scenting blood.

Gregory could not recall drawing his sword, it was just suddenly in his hand. He lashed out left and right, less interested in making kills than in staying by Richard's side. Drum reared and Gregory adjusted his seat automatically as the big horse brought his sharp hooves down on the skull of the rebel foolish enough to attempt to grab his bridle. The warhorse trampled the man's spine into the mud, just to be certain, before wheeling and snapping at the gelding carrying an axe wielding rebel. The gelding shied and fell in the slick ground, rolling on his rider before struggling away.

All hell reigned in the marketplace which had become a battlefield. Gregory knew that in a few scant moments, they would be fighting for their lives. He reined in Drum when the courser clearly wanted to go after another attacker, yanking his head towards Richard and his mount. No one had yet dared to engage the king, although Richard had his sword in hand and was controlling his horse with expert precision. Gregory had just made it back to Richard's side, when a cold prickle climbed his spine. He didn't question it. Years of surviving battlefields and skirmishes had taught him to obey his instincts. He was kneeing Drum forward to barge the king's horse even as he lifted his gaze, searching for danger. There. An archer about to loose his arrow. Richard's horse danced sideways but it wasn't enough.

Gregory flung himself out of Drum's saddle, knocking the king bodily from his horse to the ground. He felt a hot sting across his cheekbone and the outer edge of his ear and dismissed it. In the fraction of a second before he hit the ground, Gregory tried to twist and take the fall on his forearms, turning his head to the side and bending his knees slightly. He managed not to fall flat on top of Richard in full armour, but the shock of the landing travelled through his gauntleted palms up in to his shoulders. The breath exploded from his lungs. Gregory found himself half crouched over the young king who stared up at him, dark, clever eyes full of shock.

"Your face," Richard said.

Gregory felt the slow, hot trickle down his neck and sat back. "I doubt that arrow made it any worse."

Richard laughed shakily, sounding for the first time like the youth he was. "Help me up, Maudesley."

Gregory stood, shaking feeling back into numb limbs. Not as bad as a jousting fall and he'd had plenty of those. He caught the bridle of Richard's horse, which hadn't run since it was surrounded by chaos, so it couldn't decide where to run to.

"Whoa there, lad," Gregory said, pulling it firmly so that all four hooves met the earth. "Easy does it." He grasped the king by the forearm and pulled, completely overestimating how much strength he needed and almost lifting the king fully off the ground with one hand.

Richard's eyebrows rose a fraction but all he said was, "My thanks, Sir Maudesley." He boosted himself back into the saddle. No broken bones at least.

And then Gregory cursed himself because he should have been getting the king away, not presenting him as a target by putting him back on his horse. Drum shoulder barged Gregory,

133

appearing from seemingly nowhere, and he swung up onto the horse's back. He searched for the archer, then realised what Richard had already grasped. The horror at seeing the king go down had temporarily ceased the fight. Gregory kneed Drum forward before understanding why he was flanking the king.

Richard for all his youth, had not merely seen the lull in the fighting, he had understood its potential and intended to use it. The king had been fired upon and had fallen from his horse, but now here was the king, miraculously unhurt. Praise God! Richard drove his horse forward, straight at the rebel lines, crying aloud in a carrying voice.

"People of England! My people! I am your king! When you suffer, do I not also feel it?"

The mood of the crowd shifted from volatile and horrified, to strained but attentive. Richard had their attention. The young king saw this and his words gained in resonance.

"Your woes are mine. Your wounds are mine. I would heal your injuries and mend your grievances. But I cannot do so while you fight me. I say again, I am your king. I claim you as my people. What say you?"

The crowd muttered but Gregory saw hands loosen on staves and bows. Richard almost had them.

"Are you people of England? Are you mine?" Richard's clear, youthful tones rose in something like exaltation. He could scarcely be unaware of the danger and yet he held himself as if he no doubt of being obeyed. He had made the crowd feel important. He had captured them. "Let all who count themselves loyal subjects of England and the crown, go with me now. Put up your bows and clubs! Follow me, your true king!"

Gregory didn't allow himself a moment to think beyond acknowledging that the lad did indeed have a set of balls a bullock might have been proud of. And they were following him. The rebels were breaking away from the fight and falling meekly in behind the king like sheep following a shepherd. Gregory kept pace with Richard and in a few moments the rest of the guard scrambled into position around him. They looked dazed, all of them. Even Warwick. Even Standissh, who had the air of having seen everything the world had to offer and not being much moved by any of it.

Words, Gregory thought. *Mere words. And the will to command.*

The rebels followed Richard to Clerkenwell, while the remainder of the king's train brought up the rear.

18.

15th June, 1381

There was no further violence that day. It could have become a blood bath since Richard led the rebels into the surrounding forces of the militia William Walworth had raised in London. Having heard the king was in danger, the militia was eager to attack, but Richard commanded that the rebels should be allowed to depart as long as they did so peaceably. As long as they left their banners and letters patent. By that point it was known that Wat Tyler was dead. A few enterprising knights had found his cooling corpse in the priory of St Bartholomew and hacked his head off as proof. Many of the rebels knelt and begged for mercy then, either because it was politic or because they truly believed God was no longer on their side. Whatever the reason, it was the end of the revolt in London.

Richard wasted no time in setting things to rights and pressing his victory home. Philipot, Brembre, Launde and Knolles were knighted for the valour they had shown in battle, and together with Walworth, who received a royal appointment, were charged with securing the city against further incursions and breaking up riots. Once London was secure, Richard sent out men-at-arms and knights to secure the shires, to which many rebels had returned, making changes in the belief that they had the letters patent and therefore the king's blessing.

Chroniclers would later slant the truth, tweaking here, pulling there. An unvarnished tale would never do. The face of English governance had nearly been entirely overturned and such dangerously seductive ideas must be squashed, not fed. Sudbury and Hales, entered the chronicles as martyrs in everything but name. The cleverness and organisation, the very status and breadth of representation of the common folk were pared back, until the stories told were of illiterate peasants burning books for no good reason. And yet England was shaken and Europe shook with her. Never again would it be taken for granted that the commons would not rise against their tormentors.

Nor did they all go quietly back to the system they had tried so hard to break. Over the next year, Richard would be kept busy seeking pockets of resistance and stamping it out. And yet, let it not be said that the young king went back on everything he agreed at Mile End. Richard found his hands tied on the matter of villeinage and his best recourse was to empower his lords to free their villeins if they should so wish, with the assurance that they would have his full support should they choose to do so. It was little in the way of what had been promised but perhaps it was enough for now.

***

18th June, 1381

Three days after the events at Smithfield, Gregory received a summons to appear before the king at the White Tower. Westminster was still considered unsafe for official business at present and Gregory was staying as Chaucer's guest in Aldgate. He had Cuthbert saddle Drum and made an attempt with his appearance. His cheek had been laid open by the arrow aimed at the king and the stitches and swelling did little to make him look less like a ruffian. Gregory grumbled profanities and gave the matter up as a bad job.

There was no wait to see the king this time. The seneschal appeared relieved when Gregory arrived, ushering him in as if he was several hours late. Gregory scowled at the officious little man but found he wasn't really annoyed.

Richard was seated in a high backed chair, hands resting on the carved armrests, on a small dais. He waved Gregory forward when the herald announced him. Gregory stopped before the throne and dropped to one knee, bowing his head. He was dimly amused to find there was no sarcasm in the gesture. It occurred to him that for the first time in the last decade, he had finally found a man worth following. One who was clever, even handed and courageous. One who called to mind the knightly ideals he'd believed so ardently as a boy, before William had thrashed them out of him. A man who deserved Gregory's loyalty, whom he would be honoured to call king.

"Sir Maudesley," Richard said. "Please rise. I wish for an honest opinion and yours is the only one that will do."

"I am at Your Majesty's service," Gregory said. He noticed Warwick standing nearby, and Sandissh, plus a few other notables. The Earl of Oxford was in the background wearing an inscrutable expression. Warwick seemed to be struggling with a grin.

"Think you that we shall hear any more of rebellions and revolts, driven by John Ball's cant?" Richard said. "And if so, should I not crush it entirely, as several of my advisers seem to advocate?"

Gregory licked dry lips. He was never going to enjoy this sort of political wrangling. "I think, sire, that you may kill a rebellion, you may cut off its head and kill its leaders. But an idea? An idea is a very difficult thing to kill. There will be those who remember. You cannot rewrite what happened entirely." Gregory rubbed the back of his neck, realised what he was doing and snatched his hand away. "That is, Your Majesty... The Cleric, Ball, had a knack for turning a rhyme, did he not? Rhymes tend to stick in the memory. Imprison Ball, execute him, you cannot change the words he or Tyler or any of them have already spoken. And words have a power beyond that of the sword."

"Wisely spoken," Richard said. "And how, Sir Maudesley, would you address such an issue?"

Gregory stared at the king blankly for a moment but he did know. "Give them a different idea to cling to instead. And I would caution against much cruelty, begging your pardon, Your Majesty. Cruelty has its uses but clemency ought to be set beside it."

Richard smiled. "I believe you are right, Sir Maudesley.

Where possible, there shall be forgiveness. Which brings me to my second topic. I wish you to help lead the charge. Ride out. Mix cruelty with clemency, in my name."

"As you wish, sire."

"I realise you need a suitable rank. Baronet is far too low. And you need more lands to go with a new title. Maudesley estate is Wynnstree in Essex, is it not? And the mesne lord and his descendants died during the fever, so their lands and yours were returned to the Crown. Hence I am your mesne lord."

"Yes, sire," Gregory said.

"Then I shall give the mesne lord lands into your keeping. You shall be Sir Gregory Maudesley, *Baron* of Wynnstree, Lexden and Witham." Richard gave Gregory the grin of a youth and a co-conspirator. "Come, Sir Maudesley, kneel. Do you not have an oath you wish to give to your king?"

Epilogue

27th September, 1381

Gregory returned to Wynnstree in September, expecting to see out the autumn and winter months at Maudesley Castle. The nights were drawing in but an Indian summer still reigned golden over his lands. The harvest had not been such a disaster as he'd feared, and with funds from his other estates, they should all weather the cold season in relative comfort. He'd visited several times whilst on his way to or from a commission for the king. On each occasion, he'd found things further improved. Gregory knew he had his wife to thank for much of it. They had been cordial to each other on these occasions, but wary, as if unsure how far to test the fragile peace between them. Gregory thought Alienor derived a great deal of pleasure from taking such an openly active role in running his estate. His reeves and factors respected her. Even better, his commons had grown to like her, Scot or no. They *wanted* to work for Lady Maudesley. Gregory felt a twinge of envy at how easily they bridged a distance with his wife that he could not. He *had* tried.

When he'd first returned in June, Gregory had listened attentively to Alienor's account of how the flocks were fairing. Taking a steadying breath, he'd told his wife that she looked lovely. For a man who did not soften words easily, Gregory thought he'd done well. But Alienor had given him a pitying look and pointed out how little that had to do with sheep. Gregory had been glad that visit only lasted two days.

When he had stayed for a few days in August, he had not tried sweet words on her. Perhaps they worked for other men, but for Gregory, near enough thirty and growing more scarred with every skirmish, they had little effect. So he and Alienor had had long conversations that were entirely about the running of his farms and the improvements to the castle. He was surprised to find that when she wasn't using him as a whetstone for her tongue, he enjoyed talking with her, which had led him to praise her efforts. Alienor had not replied sharply that time, she had looked confused, cheeks a little pink.

"My lord, your knight!" Cuthbert exclaimed.

Gregory returned his attention to the chessboard, where Fletcher was close to checkmate, and hastily made a corrective move.

"My thanks, Master Cuthbert," Fletcher said sourly. "Have you no task you need to be about?"

"Cook said I was to shut up the hens," Cuthbert admitted.

"Be off with you then," Fletcher said. "What are you lingering in the hall for?"

Cuthbert gave a cheeky bow and ran off.

"He doesn't look a thing like the scrap I left here in spring," Gregory commented.

"My lady believes in feeding her servants," Fletcher said. "Over feeding in Cuthbert's case."

"He's a growing lad," Gregory said absently.

"If he keeps growing at his current rate, he'll have to be kept in one of the barns," Fletcher said, with no real rancour. "Ah, you have me." He looked down at the board where Gregory was forcing him into retreat.

A servant approached to say Master Fletcher was wanted elsewhere.

"Another time, my lord?" Fletcher rose stiffly.

"I'll wait, if it's a matter than can be seen to swiftly," Gregory said. He was left alone in the hall, gazing down at his goblet of wine, deep in thought. A small, white hand reached out and moved one of the chess pieces.

"Your move, my lord," Alienor said.

Gregory narrowed his eyes and moved his bishop.

Alienor retaliated. Two moves later, she took his queen.

Gregory stared at her in consternation.

Alienor smirked. "You play so aggressively, my lord. It's not always the best way to win the game."

Gregory throttled a laugh. "Are you simply in a mood to vex

me tonight, my lady? Or is there something I may do for you?"

"There is something I require," Alienor said, her cheeks reddening.

"I am at your disposal?" Gregory said uncertainly.

Alienor huffed, clearly exasperated with him though he couldn't say why. "I certainly hope so, my lord. I've come to demand my wedding rights of you." She glared at him, daring him to laugh.

Gregory's brows shot up. "Your...?"

"You're taking your own sweet time about it, I must say," Alienor said tartly. "I grew impatient with waiting."

"I see," Gregory downed his wine, then coughed, once more valiantly struggling against laughter.

Alienor was not fooled, a reluctant smile tugged at the corners of her mouth.

"Why did you agree to marry me?" The words were out before Gregory could stop them.

"It may have escaped your notice, Gregory, but I'm an active woman who likes to make improvements. Why on earth would I prefer someone who was tidy already?" Alienor laughed at his expression. "You did not seek to win me over with flattery or protestations of sentiment. My mother always said you can do far worse than an honest man."

Gregory found he was fighting a smile of his own. "You may live to regret those words before the night is out, Alienor."

"I live in hope." She pulled Gregory to his feet, and led him to up to the lord's bedchamber.

Author's Note

The King's Knight: Revolt is a work of fiction set against a backdrop of historical events. In terms of the chronology of events, I have done my best to chart the most logical course, however any reader who looks into the history further will likely find that some historians and other historical fiction authors disagree on the proper order of things. There's no way to know for certain since the chronicles detailing the Great Revolt all contradict each other to some extent. Considering the shock and upheaval caused by the events, it's hardly surprising that no one managed to write a minute by minute account of what actually happened and when.

Far from being an illiterate mob that burned books for no good reason, the rebels were a highly organised, educated and justifiably aggrieved force. Their plans for a new England and a new way of life, were not merely a departure from feudalism; they were incredibly progressive schemes for a more egalitarian country with a free market and a more socially responsible economy, conceived of centuries before the birth of socialism. The Revolt is the first event of Richard II's reign, which sees the young king emerge as a historical figure. There have been many interpretations of his actions during the revolt, some no doubt coloured by his actions later in his reign. My interpretation falls somewhere in the middle, but it would be hard to deny the courage of a fourteen-year-old boy who rode out to speak to an angry mob that had been burning down parts of London.

For those who wish to read further I highly recommend *England, Arise!* by Juliet Barker, *The Plantagenets* by Dan Jones, *The Three Richards* by Nigel Saul, *Richard II: A Brittle Glory* by Laura Ashe and *The Medieval Knight: Noble Warriors in the Golden Age of Chivalry* by Dr Phyllis G Jestice. I would be remiss if I didn't also mention the poetry of Geoffrey

Chaucer, especially *The Canterbury Tales; The Delphi Collected Poetical Works of John Gower,* especially *Confessio Amantis,* and William Langland's *Piers Ploughman.*

If you have enjoyed *The King's Knight* (or any of my other books, including *An Argument of Blood* and *A Black Matter for the King)* I would love to hear from you. You can reach me on twitter @J_AnneIronside or you can email me via jaironsideauthor@gmail.com